DESPERATE RIDE

Center Point
Large Print

Also by James J. Griffin and available from
Center Point Large Print:

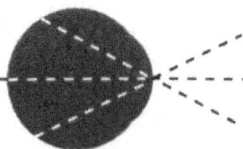

**This Large Print Book carries the
Seal of Approval of N.A.V.H.**

DESPERATE RIDE

A Texas Ranger Will Kirkpatrick Novel

JAMES J. GRIFFIN

CENTER POINT LARGE PRINT
THORNDIKE, MAINE

For Jim, Sandi, and Alice

1

Texas Ranger William Kirkpatrick was in Captain Paul Hunter's office, at Texas Ranger Headquarters in Austin. With him was his partner, a youngster by the name of Jonas Peterson.

Hunter was seated at his desk, leaning back in his chair, his feet propped up on the desk's spur-scarred, worn surface. As always, he had a cheap cigar stuck in the corner of his mouth, his third one of the work day, which was less than an hour-and-a-half old. The smoke from the cheroot filled Hunter's office with a thick, blue haze.

"Will, that was good work you did, figurin' out who was really responsible for the robbin' of your father's bank," Hunter said. "Jonas, seems like you did a fine job makin' certain the real culprit didn't make good his getaway."

"Not to mention he's makin' it a habit of savin' my bacon," Will added.

"I wasn't gonna bring that up, but now that you did, Will, if you're not careful, Jonas just might turn out to be a better lawman than you are," Hunter said.

"I dunno about that, Cap'n," Jonas answered. "I've still got a lot to learn about law work, plus don't forget, I'll also be on probation for almost another year."

Jonas had been forced into taking part in a stagecoach holdup by his two cousins, Kyle and Wylie. When Will tracked the trio down, Wylie had foolishly gone for his gun, forcing Will to shoot him dead. The next morning, when Will was preparing to transport the two surviving outlaws to Pecos, Kyle tricked him, and overpowered him with a low blow that left the Ranger paralyzed with pain.

Will was helpless when Kyle took his gun, ready to put a bullet in his chest. Jonas lunged at Kyle just as he pulled the trigger, sending his shot awry. In the ensuing struggle for Will's gun, it went off, mortally wounding Kyle. Instead of killing Will and making his escape while he had the opportunity, Jonas handed Will's gun back to him.

When Jonas stood trial, he pleaded guilty to his part in the robbery. After hearing Will's testimony about how Jonas had not only saved his life, but then refused to kill him, when he could have with no problem, the judge gave Jonas a sentence of five years, suspended, and a year's probation, in Will's custody, on the condition he join the Rangers. Jonas had agreed.

"I know you do, son, but you're off to an excellent start," Hunter said. "Will, I'm happy to hear you patched things up with your family, too. That's important."

"Thanks, Cap'n. My folks still don't approve

of me bein' a Ranger, but at least now they understand I had to follow my own path."

"Speaking of which, I assume you boys are ready to hit the trail again," Hunter said.

"Boy howdy, I should say so," Will answered. "Where're you sendin' us, Cap'n?"

"My original intention was to have you rejoin your company," Hunter answered. "However, circumstances have changed that. I need you back out in west Texas."

"Any particular man we'll be huntin' for?"

"Nope. It seems like there's more than the usual run of bandits, con artists, and just plain bad men runnin' roughshod all over that territory."

"Organized bunch?" Jonas asked.

"That's a fair question, but they don't appear to be," Hunter answered. "Most of the crimes seem to be committed against isolated ranches, stagecoaches, or small settlements. You know how it is, especially in Texas. Too much land for desperadoes to hide in, and far too few lawmen to run 'em down. Word gets around about easy pickings, so more and more renegades show up. The few honest folks who might try'n stand up to 'em are gunned down or burned out. The ones left are too scared to try'n stop 'em, with good reason. I thought about sending a troop in there, but that many men would be noticed too easy. The bad guys would just disappear into thc tall and uncut, wait until the troop moved on, then start their depredations all over again. That's where you two come in."

"You mind explainin' that, Cap'n?" Will asked.

"I'm about to, if you'll stop interrupting and let me," Hunter answered. "I need a couple of men who can drift into a place without anyone suspectin' they're Rangers. While I've got a dozen or so who fit the bill, right now, you two are the only ones available. All the others already have assignments. Will, you're still pretty young lookin', and Jonas, I reckon I don't have to tell you again you damn for certain don't look old enough to be a Ranger. Hell, you still can't hardly grow a decent crop of whiskers. You'll be able to nose around without anyone even payin' attention."

"So you want us to just kind of mosey around the countryside, arresting the *malo hombres* wherever we happen to find 'em," Jonas said.

"Well, I hope you'll move at a faster pace than just moseyin', but yes, that's the general idea," Hunter answered.

"Any particular place you'd like us to start, Cap'n?" Will asked.

"Yup. I couldn't wrangle any tickets on the M-K-T Railroad for you from here to Fort Worth, so you'll make that part of the journey on horseback. Shouldn't take you more'n five days. Once you reach Fort Worth, you'll take a Texas and Pacific train to Sweetwater. There'll be a cattle car for your horses. Soon as you reach Sweetwater, you'll start there. Check in with Sheriff Butler. He's a good man. After that, it doesn't matter to me which direction you head, nor how far, long as you round up as many owlhoots as you can find. And I shouldn't have to tell you, if they put up a fight, don't worry about takin' prisoners."

"Ridin' hard, it won't take us more'n four days to reach Forth Worth, Cap'n," Will said.

"Even better. You can start out first thing tomorrow mornin'. For today, pick up whatever supplies you need, make certain your horses are ready for a long run, then take the rest of the day off and get a good night's shut-eye."

"Neither one of us'll argue with that," Will said. "Anythin' else?"

"Just be careful, and good luck."

"Okay. Let's get goin', Jonas. *Adios*, Cap'n."

"*Adios*," Jonas added.

"*Vaya con Dios*, both of you. Keep in touch by mail, unless something's so urgent you need to send a telegram."

"Understood, Cap'n," Will said. "See you when the job is done."

2

"We'll cross the Brazos at Waco, then get a room for the night," Will said, two days later. "Should hit the bridge a couple of hours before sundown."

"There's a bridge over the Brazos?" Jonas asked.

"There damn for certain is. You've never been to Waco?"

"No, I can't say as I have."

"It's a wild town. The Chisolm Trail passes right through it, so there's lots of saloons and gamblin' places that are more than willing to take trail hands' money. As for the bridge, it's been there quite a few years now. I've used it many times. It sure is a lot easier to manage than the old ferry, or findin' a ford. The Brazos is tricky. It can be calm, or have a mighty fast current. There's quicksand and deep holes to worry about. That's not even mentioning the cottonmouths."

"Snakes? I hate snakes. I'd rather face a horde of war-crazed Apaches."

"That makes two of us, pardner. Let's pick up the pace."

Will spurred Pete, his close-coupled black and white overo paint, into a long-legged lope. Jonas and Rebel, his blaze-faced bay gelding, matched them stride for stride.

• • •

"It won't be long now, Jonas," Will said, three hours later. "You see that squarish lookin' object poking up over the trees?"

Will pointed to the tip of a structure, which was illuminated by the late afternoon sun.

"Yeah, Will. Just barely."

"Well, it won't look so small right soon. That's one of the towers that hold up the bridge. You won't believe your own eyes when you see how massive it is. We'll be crossing the Brazos in less than thirty minutes."

"What're we gonna do once we get into town?"

"Jonas, for a kid who seems so smart, that was a downright dumb question," Will answered, with a short laugh. "First, we'll put up our horses. Then, we'll get us a room, so we can clean up a bit. After that, we'll eat supper, then have a few drinks. I plan on lookin' up a certain lady I'm rather fond of, too. Hope she's still around."

When they reached the Waco Suspension Bridge, Jonas pulled Rebel to a sudden stop.

"*That's* the bridge you've been talkin' about, Will? We're supposed to ride across that thing?"

"Sure. There's nothin' to it. I've used this bridge lots of times. The company behind the design is building an even bigger one, way up in New York City."

"There's not a chance in Hell you'll get me to

ride out on that bridge," Jonas said, with a shake of his head. "It'll collapse right under us. Look at those itty-bitty strings holdin' that contraption up."

"Those aren't strings. Those are thick steel cables," Will answered. "The towers are solid brick, three million bricks. Like I've already told you, I've used this bridge quite a few times. It's a lot safer'n swimmin' the river, or tryin' the old ferry that still runs, and maybe capsizing and drownin'."

"I'm not buyin' that story, Will."

"Listen, Jonas. The Chisholm Trail runs right through here. We're on it right now. Hundreds of cattle herds, with cows numberin' in the thousands, cross this bridge every year, on their way to the railheads in Kansas. Hell, if they can cross this bridge, two men on horses can damn sure cross it."

"Seems like we won't have to worry about it," Jonas said. "The gates are down. Reckon the bridge must be closed. That's a pity. I guess we'll just have to go around."

"The bridge ain't closed," Will answered. "It's a toll bridge. You have to pay to cross it. But since we're lawmen, we use it for free. All we have to do is show the gate keeper our papers. Get your commission out, pardner."

Will pulled his billfold from his hip pocket and removed his Ranger commission. Jonas shook his head, but did the same. When they rode up to the gate, the bridge keeper emerged from his house.

"Howdy, gents," he said. "Fixin' to cross? It's five cents apiece for horses and riders."

"We're Texas Rangers," Will answered. He and Jonas handed their commissions to the bridge keeper. The man examined the papers, then handed them back.

"Those seem in order. Go right ahead."

Will and Jonas waited for the keeper to open the gate. Once it was, they put their horses into a walk. Pete walked readily onto the bridge. Rebel stopped at the edge of the deck, snorting. He danced sideways when Jonas spurred him forward.

"C'mon, Rebel, you damn jughead," Jonas yelled.

"Tap him on his rump with the reins," Will suggested.

"All right."

Jonas slapped his reins on Rebel's rump. The bay stepped onto the bridge's wooden deck. As soon as he felt the wood vibrating under his front hooves, he reared, spun on his back heels, came down, and bolted. Jonas had to haul back hard, sawing on the reins, until he got his horse back under control. Will and Pete waited on the bridge, watching the show, along with the bridge keeper.

Jonas stopped Rebel before he stepped onto the bridge deck again.

"Rebel don't like this here bridge a'tall." Jonas

shook his head. "I don't much blame him."

"He's picking up on your nervousness," Will answered. "Take a couple of deep breaths, to calm yourself down. Once your horse realizes you're not afraid, he'll be more confident. He's got to know he can trust you, and that you won't put him into a spot that's not safe. You've got to trust him, too."

"We trust each other," Jonas shot back, "But neither one of us trusts this damn bridge. That's for damn certain."

"It's either this bridge or a long detour," Will answered. "And if you don't trust the bridge, I'd wager my hat you'd never get on a river ferry, let alone your horse. What's it gonna be?"

Jonas lifted his hat to wipe sweat from his brow. He shook his head, then jammed the hat back in place.

"Let's go, Rebel."

He urged the bay gelding onto the bridge, once again. This time, Rebel got about ten feet onto the deck before stopping. He stood, trembling, the whites of his eyes showing his fear.

"Keep him right behind me'n Pete," Will advised. "He'll follow us, once he sees Pete ain't scared. He's not gonna want to stay behind, by himself. Or would you rather I tie a lead to him and pull him along?"

"No. He wouldn't stand for that. I'll get him movin'."

Jonas dug his spurs into Rebel's sides. Rebel tossed his head, but began moving. He walked slowly, lifting his hooves high with each step, almost prancing. He rolled his eyes every time the wooden deck rumbled hollowly under his feet, or those of other passing riders.

When they reached the far side of the bridge, the armpits of Jonas's gray wool shirt were darkened with perspiration, which also soaked the shirt's chest and plastered it to his back. Rebel was lathered with sweat.

"See," Will said. "Nothin' to it. Next time you won't have any problems at all."

"There'd better not be a next time," Jonas said. "Where to now?"

"Well, pardner, lookin' at you and your horse, we're headin' straight for a livery stable to get him cooled down and brushed out. After that, we'll get that room so we can clean up a bit. You for certain can't wear that shirt to any decent restaurant. We'll drop off our dirty duds at a Chinese laundry for cleaning."

Three hours later, Will and Jonas were standing on the boardwalk in front of the Wagon Wheel Café, smoking. They had just finished their suppers of steak, boiled potatoes, black-eyed peas, and pecan pie, washed down with strong black coffee.

"Where are we goin' now, Will?" Jonas asked.

"We're headed to Rose's La Vie en Rouge," Will answered.

"La Vie en Rouge? What the hell is that?"

"You'll see when we get there. That's where I first met Simone. I can promise you one thing. You'll like the place. It's only a few minutes from here. Let's go."

After a short walk, the two Rangers reached the intersection of Dallas and Tyler Streets, two of the busiest Waco thoroughfares on the north side of the Brazos. On the southwest corner stood a three-story limestone building, painted a dusky red. A verandah ran the full length of the building's street sides. Red glass globed wall sconces were placed every five feet along the walls, illuminating the verandah and boardwalk with a scarlet glow. A sign hung diagonally from the verandah's corner. In the center of the sign was painted a large red rose. The line above the rose, done in a florid script, proclaimed the establishment as "Mme. Rose's La Vie en Rouge." Underneath the rose another line read "Exclusive Club for Gentlemen of Distinction, Taste, and Refinement." They reined up in front and dismounted.

"*This* is where you're takin' me, Will?" Jonas exclaimed, looking at the structure.

"Sure is. Why? Somethin' wrong?"

"Yeah. You might consider yourself a gentleman, comin' from a wealthy family and all, but I sure ain't one, let alone a gentleman of distinction. I come from a family of hard-scrabble, dirt poor farmers. Only reason I'm not in jail is you stuck up for me in front of the judge, and put in a good word for me with the cap'n. This place is too dang high-falutin' for the likes of me."

"No, it's not," Will answered. "It's lots nicer than most establishments of this type, but Mademoiselle Rose caters to just about anyone. Long as you don't stir up trouble, and don't get too drunk, or rough with the girls, Rose will be happy to provide your entertainment."

"That's another thing, Will. Girls?"

"What's botherin' you about girls?"

"I've—well, that is, I . . ."

Jonas's voice trailed off. He blushed deep red, almost as red as the rose on the sign.

"Wait a minute, Jonas. Are you tryin' to tell me you ain't never been with a woman?"

Jonas's face turned even redder. He dragged the toe of his left boot through the dirt.

"I . . . Aw, hell. No, Will. I kissed Becky Sue Jackson behind the schoolhouse once, but that's all. Never had the courage to do anythin' more."

"Then it's high time you learn about women. Let's get inside," Will said, as he tied Pete to the rail.

"I . . . I dunno, Will."

"Look, no one's gonna force you to do anythin' you don't want to. If you're not ready, that's all right. Just come with me, have a couple of drinks, and we'll see what happens."

"Okay."

"*Mon Dieu*! Will Kirkpatrick! As I live and breathe! *Bonsoir, mon amour.* It has been too long," the woman behind the front desk shouted, as soon as she saw Will and Jonas. "And you've grown a moustache. It looks *tres bien* on you, *mon cheri.*"

"Mademoiselle" Rose Chantal spoke in a French accent, which was as phony as the color of the peroxide blonde hair piled high on her head, then pulled back in curls at the nape of her neck. She was a buxom woman, somewhere in her late thirties to early forties, a bit heavier these days, but still attractive. Her eyes were a deep shade of blue, almost violet. She wore a form-fitting, full length scarlet satin gown, cut low to show off her bosom to best advantage.

Her name was as phony as her accent. Rose Chantal was born plain old Maggie Collier in Baton Rouge, Louisiana. She was the fourth of seven children, all girls. Her father was a dock worker on the Mississippi River, loading and unloading cargo from the steamboats which plied the river, and pulled into port at Baton Rouge. He was a hard-drinking man, who regularly beat his wife and daughters. Her mother took in laundry to supplement the family's meager income.

At fourteen, tired of her father's abuse and living in poverty, Maggie left home. She soon found work in the Chateau Bleu, one of the many riverfront brothels that catered to sailors and dock workers. The man who ran the establishment changed her name to Rose, and taught her how to speak rudimentary French.

When she was sixteen, one of the Chateau Bleu's clients, Henri Deschamps, paid enough to take her with him to New Orleans. He established his own house of ill-repute, making Rose the madam, or manager, as he preferred she be known, and taking her as his lover. The enterprise was a thriving success, until the night Rose found Deschamps *in flagrante delicto* with one of the working girls. Two shots from Rose's Derringer, one bullet each into Deschamps' and the woman's foreheads, ended their lives.

Rose was forced to flee Louisiana to avoid murder charges. She made her escape across the Sabine River and into Texas, where she eventually worked her way to Waco. Realizing that servicing cowhands driving cattle north along the Chisholm Trail from Texas to Kansas could be every bit as lucrative as plying her trade with river men, Rose set up a small brothel. Within two years, her business had grown into "La Vie en Rouge."

She charged more for her services than in the average sporting house, but the customers were happy to pay the difference for the upgraded liquor at her bar, the cleanliness of the house, and the fake French atmosphere.

"Howdy, Rose," Will answered. "You're right, it has been too long since I've spent time in Waco."

"But you are here now. That's all that matters. Who is your *jeune ami*?"

"This here's Jonas Peterson. He's my new riding pard. Jonas, stop being rude. Put your eyes back in their sockets, and say howdy to Mademoiselle Rose."

Jonas was gazing at all the details of the La Vie en Rouge—the heavy crimson brocaded drapes covering the windows, the scarlet tapestries on the walls, the gilt and red crystal chandeliers, the ornately carved red rugs, the red velvet sofas and chairs. Mostly, he was staring at the women, of all shapes, sizes, ages, and colors, lounging on those sofas. Every one of them was in a red dress.

"I-I'm sorry, ma'am," he said. "Howdy."

"Ma'am . . . You make me sound like *une vieille femme*."

Rose came from behind the desk. She walked up to Jonas, and stood with her cleavage directly under his nose. Lamplight glinted off the large ruby which nestled there.

"Now, do I look like an old woman?"

"No, ma'am. You sure don't. Not one bit."

"Then stop addressing me as one, my *bon ami*. You may call me Mademoiselle, or Rose, whichever you prefer. Now, kiss my hand, *s'il vous plait*."

Rose extended her hand.

"Well?"

"Yes'm."

Jonas blushed, took her hand, and barely brushed his lips against it.

"*Mon juene ami*, I can see you have little knowledge in the ways of *amour*," Rose said.

"No, mademoiselle. I sure don't."

"Jonas has never been in a place like this," Will explained.

"Ah, I understand. You have come to the right place to learn, Jonas. I will personally make certain you enjoy your time at La Vie en Rouge."

"Rose, aren't you forgetting someone?" Will asked.

"*Sacre bleu*! *Moi*? Forget *anyone*, let alone *you*, Will?" Rose answered. "Heaven forbid."

"In that case, I'm kinda hopin' Simone is still here," Will said.

"Simone. Of course, she is here. She is one of my best girls, as you well know. She will be very glad to see you again. However, she does not begin work for another hour."

"I can wait," Will said.

"Excellent. As for you, Jonas, I am going to have Genevieve take care of your needs," Rose said. "She is very experienced at teaching first-time lovers. You will enjoy her company, very much indeed. I will arrange for her to meet you the same time Simone and Will visit. Until then, why don't the two of you wait at the bar? I'll have the ladies meet you there. The first drink is on the house, as always."

"That's a fine idea, Rose," Will said. "Follow me, Jonas. The barroom is right this way. Rose, we'll see the ladies in about an hour."

"Simone and Genevieve will be ready."

"*Merci.*"

Will led Jonas into the barroom. Since it was still relatively early, the space wasn't crowded.

"Will Kirkpatrick," the lady behind the bar called, when she saw him. "Where the devil have you been keepin' yourself? It's been ages."

Will grinned.

"The Rangers keep me on the go, Madge darlin'. In fact, we're just passin' through. We'll only be in town for tonight. I'd like you to meet my new pardner, Jonas Peterson. Jonas, this here's Madge Stanley. She's been tendin' bar here as long as I can remember."

Madge was anywhere from her late sixties to early eighties. She stood no more than four feet ten inches tall. She was slight, probably weighing ninety pounds soaking wet. Silver hair encircled her face, in which was set deep green eyes. She wore a black silk gown, embroidered with red roses on the bust and hips.

"My, he's a young one, ain't he?" Madge said, running her gaze over Jonas's lean form. "Hope you enjoy your visit, sonny. Will, what're you havin' to drink?"

"My usual, Madge."

"One bottle of Old Grand-Dad, right. Jonas, what's your pleasure? I'm afraid we don't have any sarsaparilla, or milk."

"I'll have the same as my pardner . . . ma'am."

Will broke into laughter.

"He got you there, Madge," he said. "You've just been 'ma'amed'."

"I suppose it serves me right," Madge said, laughing herself. "All right, Jonas. If you're man enough to be a Ranger, I reckon you're man enough to drink red-eye."

She rummaged under the bar, came up with two bottles of whiskey and two glasses. Will tossed three silver dollars on the mahogany.

"I've got the drinks, Jonas."

"I'm obliged, Will. *Gracias.*"

They each filled a glass, and downed the first drink in one quick swallow.

"Not bad at all," Jonas said.

"I told you this was a nice place," Will answered. He filled his glass again, this time sipping at the contents.

25

"We might as well take our time and enjoy this red-eye," he said. "The ladies won't be here for a spell."

Will and Jonas spent the next hour working on their drinks. The whiskey bottles were nearly empty when Rose returned. With her were two other women. The first one, a tall, willowy, blue-eyed strawberry blonde, who wore a gold and crimson gown almost exactly the color of her hair, walked straight up to Will and kissed him full on the lips.

"Well, it's about time you showed up again," she said.

"Howdy, Simone. It *has* been too long," Will answered. "But I'd never forget your kiss."

"You're lucky it wasn't a slap, since you've kept me waiting for months," Simone Robineau answered. "I shouldn't even speak to you."

"You know I have to go where the Rangers send me, darlin'."

"You could have somehow made the time to get back to Waco before now."

"Jonas, while those two lovebirds have their reunion, allow me to introduce you to Genevieve Rousseau," Rose said. "Genevieve, this young man is Jonas Peterson. I promised that you would provide him an unforgettable evening."

"You did not tell me he had blonde hair and blue eyes," Genevieve said. "*J'adore* men with blonde hair and blue eyes. This will be most pleasurable."

Genevieve was a few inches shorter than Simone, but more fully-figured. She had long black hair, worn straight. Dark brown eyes and high cheekbones highlighted her oval face. Her skin was the color of café au lait, hinting at the Creole blood running through her veins, with perhaps a touch of African or Indian mixed in. Her dress was a deep shade of pink. She spoke with a soft, deep southern Louisiana accent.

"Bonsoir, Monsieur Jonas," Genevieve said. "It's a pleasure to meet you."

Jonas tipped his hat to her.

"Howdy, Miss Rousseau."

"Jonas, if we are to be *amis*, call me Genevieve, *s'il vous plait*."

She drifted her hands across his chest.

"Yes'm, I mean, Genevieve."

"That's better."

"Will, would you and your friend want another drink before we go upstairs?" Rose asked.

"I can't say for Jonas, but speaking for myself, I've had plenty to drink," Will answered.

"I've had enough whiskey for tonight," Jonas said.

"Excellent. Then *laissez le bon temps rouler*," Simone said.

"What's that mean?" Jonas asked.

"It means let the good times roll," Genevieve

answered. "Come with me and you'll see exactly what Simone is talking about."

Jonas blushed, and swallowed hard.

"All right, I reckon."

"This way."

Genevieve led Jonas up the stairs, across the gallery encircling the bar, and to a room seven doors down. Simone and Will trailed behind, but went into a room two doors before Genevieve's.

Will and Simone were back downstairs. They were in the bar, sharing the remaining whiskey left in Will's bottle, while they waited for Jonas and Genevieve. The barroom was much more crowded than earlier.

"Your *jeune ami* must really be enjoying Genevieve's company," Simone said.

"I reckon," Will answered. "Or mebbe they're just having a real interesting conversation. I wonder how much longer they'll be?"

"Here they come now," Simone said. "I think your friend had a good time. Look at the smile on his face."

Jonas and Genevieve were almost halfway down the stairs, walking side by side. One of three cowboys drinking at a table spotted them. He jumped up so quickly his chair tipped over.

"Genevieve! I meant what I said when I swore I'd see you dead before I ever let you take another man, again. You're my gal."

"Judd Hoover, I'm not any one man's girl. I told you that when you tried to take me away and force me to marry you, last time you were in. You were drunk then, and I figured once you sobered up, you'd come to your senses. Go back to your whiskey, or bother one of the other girls, you *cochon*."

"I'm gonna kill you, bitch, and the bastard with you."

Hoover grabbed for his gun.

Jonas shoved Genevieve aside, then jumped over the banister feet first. His heavy boots slammed into Hoover's chest just as he pulled the trigger. Hoover's bullet punched through the wall where Genevieve had been standing.

Jonas's impact knocked Hoover to the floor, his momentum causing him to continue on, off-balance. He hit the floor, rolled over, and scrambled back to where Hoover lay in the sawdust. He grabbed Hoover's shirtfront, intending to smash a punch to his jaw. However, Hoover was already out cold. His head hung limply. Blood flowed from his ears, and a pink froth bubbled from his lips. His breastbone and three ribs were broken, pieces of bone puncturing his heart and a lung. He had only a few minutes to live.

One of Hoover's partners pulled his six-gun, and aimed it at Jonas's back. Will pulled his own gun, and shot him in the stomach. The man's arm dropped to his side. His gun fell from his hand. He stood there, not moving, staring vacantly into space. Will kept his gun aimed at the man, ready to shoot him again. After a moment, the cowboy dropped into a chair. Only the red stain spreading across his shirt gave any indication he was gravely wounded.

A shotgun blasted its deep-throated road. Hoover's other partner staggered, then fell, his back riddled with rock salt and horseshoe nails.

"Don't anybody else move, less'n you want to get your hide ventilated too. I've still got one barrel left," Madge warned, from behind the bar. Smoke curled from the Greener she held. The gun looked heavier than Madge herself, but she held it steady, her aim unwavering. She pointed at two of the men in the barroom.

"Charlie, go get Doc Morrison. Herb, find the marshal, or one of his deputies."

"You all right, Jonas?" Will asked. Smoke still curled from the barrel of the Colt in his hand.

"Yeah, I'm okay."

"What about that *hombre*?"

"He's done for, Will. I'm gonna check on Genevieve."

"Go ahead. Madge'n I have things under control."

Genevieve was sitting at the bottom of the staircase, pain on her face. One of the other women was with her.

"Genevieve, I'm sorry I had to do that," Jonas said. "How bad are you hurt?"

"It's only a twisted ankle," Madeleine, the woman with her, answered. "She'll be just fine."

"There is no need to apologize, Jonas, *mon cheri*," Genevieve assured him. "If you had not shoved me aside, I would be dead. Is Judd—"

"He's done for," Jonas answered. "He won't be bothering you anymore. Nobody else, neither."

"Good." Genevieve spat at Hoover's body. "He was a loco *cochon*."

Rose had hurried from the front, and was now standing with Will. She was unfazed by the carnage, worried only about her girls.

"What started all this, Will?"

Will pointed his pistol toward Hoover's body.

"That *hombre* lyin' dead over there. He threatened to kill Miss Genevieve. Jonas stopped him. When one of his pards tried to back-shoot Jonas, I gut-shot him. He's the *hombre* in the chair. Don't know if he's still alive or not. Madge took care of the third *hombre* before he could plug me."

"Like the Ranger says, Judd tried to kill me, Rose," Genevieve added. "But thanks to Jonas's courage, I merely have a twisted ankle, and some bruises from my fall."

"Judd Hoover? I told him if he started trouble one more time he'd never be allowed in here again," Rose said. "I guess I should have just

31

thrown him out and told him not to come back last visit he made."

"Well, I can guarantee you that he won't make any more trouble," Will said with a grim smile. "Neither will his pardners."

Herb returned, accompanied by a lanky young man wearing a deputy marshal's badge on his cowhide vest, and carrying a rifle.

"Found Deputy Solis already on his way. He heard the shots. I saw Charlie with the doc a few buildings down. They'll be here any minute."

Deputy Marshal Joe Solis looked straight at Will, who still had his pistol at the ready.

"You mind handin' over that gun, mister?" he said. "Then you can explain to me just what the hell happened here."

"It's Ranger. Texas Ranger Will Kirkpatrick. That's my pard Jonas Peterson on the stairs. I reckon I'll just hang on to my pistol if you don't mind, Deputy . . . or even if you do."

Solis hesitated, as if he was considering challenging Will. He shrugged, realizing Will could put a bullet through him before he even got his rifle level. And if he did somehow manage to shoot Will, Jonas would be certain to drop him where he stood.

"Seein' as you're a Ranger, I guess it'll be okay. Long as you've got a good reason for gunnin' down three men."

Before Jonas could answer, Charlie came

through the door. Trailing him was a young, blonde-haired, blue-eyed man carrying a black medical bag. He quickly took in the situation.

"Are all these men dead?" he asked.

"The two on the floor sure are," Will said. "Dunno about the *hombre* in the chair. He was still breathin', last I checked."

"I'll get to work, then."

The physician went over to the wounded cowboy and felt for a pulse.

"He's still alive, but I don't know for how much longer. I can't do anything for him here. I need a couple of men to carry him to my office. With a lot of luck, I might be able to pull him through."

"Charlie, Herb, you might as well lend Doc Morrison a hand, since you've already started," Rose ordered. "There'll be a bottle on the house for each of you. And Doc, when you're finished with him, I'll need you to return and check Genevieve's injuries. There'll be a bottle waiting for you, also. My finest sherry."

Morrison nodded.

"One of you might as well go for the undertaker while you're at it," Solis said.

"Right, Deputy," Herb answered.

"Now, Ranger, you were about to tell me what started this ruckus," Solis said. "And why three men ended up full of lead."

"Actually, only one man took a bullet, the

one that Doc's working on," Will said. "This whole thing started over a woman. Jonas had just finished visiting Miss Genevieve, when that *hombre* lyin' over there, with the caved-in chest, said he was gonna kill both of 'em. Claimed Genevieve was his woman, and no one else's. Before he could make good on his threat, Jonas jumped the rail and landed on the son of a bitch. Must've busted up his insides, because he died right quick, with a lot of blood comin' out of his mouth and nose. He got off one shot. You can see the bullet hole in the wall, right where Jonas and Miss Genevieve were standin'. It was self-defense. If Jonas hadn't stopped him, that *hombre* would've killed both him and Genevieve."

"It was Judd Hoover, Joe," Rose said. "He never was good for anything. Neither were the two with him."

"I can see who it is," Solis answered. "Let the Ranger finish."

"The *hombre* who's still alive pulled his gun and tried to shoot my pard in the back," Will continued. "So I plugged him."

"It's Jim Tenney," Madge broke in. "And Hank Tobias was the third one. He was goin' to shoot Will, there. So I grabbed ol' Morton and *I* plugged *him.* I peppered him good with rock salt and horseshoe nails. Works just as good as buckshot, and a helluva lot cheaper."

Solis looked around the room.

"Anyone who was here see what happened differently?"

He was answered with a murmur of "no's" and a shaking of heads.

"All right, Ranger. I reckon I won't have to take you or your pardner down to the jail for more questions, mebbe hold y'all on suspicion of murder. You neither, Madge. However, you Rangers, you'll have to stay in town until the inquest. Probably be three-four days before we can put a coroner's jury together."

Will shook his head.

"I'm sorry, Deputy, but I'm afraid we can't do that. We're on our way to west Texas, to put a stop to some tall trouble boilin' over out there. We'll be movin' on at sunup tomorrow. We'll give you our statements tonight, right here. If you need more information later, get a message to Captain Paul Hunter at Ranger Headquarters in Austin. He'll get it to us."

"I dunno if I can let you do that," Solis objected.

"I'm not givin' you a choice in the matter," Will answered.

"Joe, we all know what happened," Rose said. "If you want to keep enjoying your free 'benefits' here at my place, you need to let this drop, right now. Or would you prefer I let Marshal Davies know a certain *gendarme* is interfering with my affairs? I'm certain you are aware he would not be pleased."

Solis's face flushed. He swallowed hard.

"No, Mademoiselle Rose, I'm sure he wouldn't be. Ranger, soon as I have you and your pardner's statements, you'll be free to go."

"I appreciate that, Deputy."

Once their statements were written out and signed, and after making their *au revoir*s to Rose, Simone, and Genevieve, Will and Jonas returned to their hotel. They requested an extra pitcher of hot water, and a basin, which they took to their room.

"You mind if I clean up first, Will?" Jonas asked, as he lit the lamp, while Will closed the door.

"No, you go ahead. I've got to clean my gun. I'll do that while you wash up. It'll take me a while, anyway."

"*Gracias.*"

Jonas trimmed the lamp's wick, then sat on the edge of the bed. He pulled off his boots and socks, then peeled out of his shirt.

"You want the window open, Will?"

"Yeah. It's a mite stuffy in here."

" 'A mite' is putting it mildly."

Jonas opened the window. A slight breeze stirred the air. He padded over to the washstand, picked up a bar of soap and washcloth. He used the hot water to scrub his hair, face, neck, upper torso, and feet. After toweling off, he washed out his shirt and socks in the basin, then draped them over the windowsill to dry.

"You might want to take your wash, and finish cleanin' your gun afterwards," he told Will. "Your water's coolin' off."

"I'm just about finished," Will answered. "It'll still be warm some. Those pitchers are mighty thick. They hold the heat."

"Suit yourself."

Jonas stretched out on the bed, lying on his back. He put his hands behind his head, gazed at the ceiling, and let out a deep sigh.

"You all right, Jonas?" Will asked.

"Yeah, I'm just fine."

"That sigh sure didn't sound like it. What's botherin' you?"

"Nothin', Will. Just thinkin' back on the day, that's all. I mean, when I was with Genevieve, it was the most pleasure I've ever felt in my life. Almost as if I'd died and gone to Paradise. Then, only a few minutes later, I have to kill a man. Talk about goin' from high to low. Crazy, ain't it?"

"Life can be plumb loco, that's for certain," Will said. "And thinkin' too hard on it could make *you* plumb loco. Me, too, for that matter. You need to talk about tonight?"

"No, I just need some shut-eye," Jonas

answered. He yawned, then rolled onto his belly. "Just don't wake me up when you slide under the sheet. G'night, Will."

"I won't be much longer. 'Night."

3

"We made good time the past couple of days, Jonas," Will said. "We should be in Fort Worth by early afternoon tomorrow. That'll give us, and our horses, time to rest and put on the feedbag before we have to catch our train."

Jonas glanced at the sky.

"The sun'll be down in about an hour. You have any idea where to set up camp tonight?"

"Yup, there's a creek about half-a-mile ahead. We'll stop early, and spend the night there. Good grazin' for the horses, and some oaks we can sleep under. I've used the spot a couple of times. It's better'n a lot of hotels I've stayed in."

"Don't take much to beat most of 'em," Jonas answered.

"That's for dang sure," Will agreed. "C'mon, Pete, pick up those hooves."

"You too, Rebel."

They kicked their weary mounts into a trot.

Once they reached the creek, Will and Jonas allowed their horses a long drink, then dismounted.

"It's a doggone shame we won't have a night to spend in Fort Worth before we have to get on our train," Jonas said, as he removed the saddle and blanket from Rebel's back.

"Well, we *could* miss the train," Will answered, grinning.

"That'd probably get us in Dutch with Cap'n Hunter," Jonas said.

"There ain't no probably about it, unless we had a damn good excuse, which we don't."

Jonas took a piece of hardtack from his saddlebag, and gave it to Rebel.

"Well, at least we won't be in the saddle for a few days. It's gotta be what, three-four days to Sweetwater?"

"Depends. If everything goes perfect, it'll only be two days, mebbe a bit less. That all depends on how many stops the train we get makes between here and Sweetwater, plus how many people are ridin' it. But you're right, the train'll be easier on our butts than sittin' on a horse for the next two hundred miles. More important, it'll give the horses a rest, too. If things are as bad where we're headed as the cap'n claims, Pete and Rebel will need to be fresh when we get there. Last thing we'd need is worn out horses, if we got into a runnin' chase with a band of desperadoes."

"Why, I heard tell the folks where we're headed are downright friendly, Will. Real peaceable and law-abiding, too. Upstanding citizens, each and every one. Who welcome lawmen with open arms."

"You just go ahead and keep tellin' yourself that, Jonas. You know what it'll get you?"

"A nice meal, fine whiskey, and a good lookin' woman to keep me company?"

"I can't say for certain about the last two, but you'll get your belly filled, all right. Filled with lead."

Pete snorted, and buried his muzzle in Will's stomach.

"What's the matter, pal? You don't like my jokes? Or do you just want a biscuit?"

Pete bobbed his head.

"All right, you can have your danged biscuit."

Will pulled a leftover biscuit from his saddlebag and gave it to the paint.

"Happy now? You mind if I finish brushin' you?"

Pete snorted and shook his head.

"Too bad. You're getting the sweat and dirt scraped off of you anyway, horse."

After caring for their horses, then picketing them to graze, Will and Jonas ate their own supper of bacon, beans, and biscuits, washed down with bitter black coffee. They had final cigarettes, then unrolled their bedrolls and crawled under their blankets.

Something awakened Jonas several hours later. The moon had set, leaving only the dim light of the stars. Jonas listened as he peered into the darkness, straining to see or hear whatever had disturbed his slumber. He glanced at Will, as he slid his six-gun out of the holster next to him. Hs partner appeared to still be asleep.

As Jonas tried to figure out what had jolted him awake, he looked at the horses. Both were standing stock still, heads high and ears pricked sharply forward. Rebel gave a soft, nervous whicker. Jonas now realized what had awoken him. Someone was trying to sneak up on the camp, apparently attempting to steal the Rangers' horses. He could hear the night creatures go silent, then resume their chirpings and buzzing as the person passed their hiding spots.

Following the silence, Jonas could see grass rustling as the intruder made his approach. He lifted his pistol and tracked the person's progress. At a spot where the grass thinned out, he was able to see the silhouette of a man, crawling along on his belly. Jonas aimed and fired. He was rewarded with a yelp of pain. The intruder rolled over, and scrambled back into deeper cover. Jonas sent another bullet at him, uncertain if he hit his target.

Jolted awake by the gunfire, Will grabbed his Colt and scrambled to his hands and knees.

"What the Hell?" he exclaimed.

"Someone was sneakin' up on us. I think he was tryin' to steal our horses. I took a shot at him," Jonas answered.

"You hit him?" Will asked.

"I'm pretty sure I did. After I shot, he gave a

yell, then ducked back into the brush. Dunno how bad he's hit."

"Why didn't you try'n wake me up?"

"Didn't want to scare him off. Also, there wasn't enough time. You reckon we should try'n find him?"

A rataplan of hoof beats, moving fast, came through the still night air, quickly fading away.

"That answers your question," Will said. "Reckon he's not hurt bad enough he couldn't get back to his horse and ride off. Probably wouldn't have been a good idea anyway. He could have laid in wait for us, and picked us off real easy. Let's settle the horses, then try'n get some more shut-eye. We'll see if we can pick up his trail come sunup. Damn."

"What's wrong, Will?"

"I can't believe I was sleepin' so sound I let an *hombre* get that close. I dang sure won't make that mistake again. Lucky you heard him."

"I reckon," Jonas said. "No harm done."

When they went to retrieve their horses the next morning, Will pointed to a large, brownish-red stain in the grass.

"Look there, Jonas. That's blood. Seems like you got him pretty good. Let's see if we can find where he had his horse."

"Sure thing."

"He went off this way."

43

A trail of broken, bent grass and brush marked the would-be horse thief's return path. Rather than going in a straight line, it weaved back and forth.

"Looks like the *hombre* was staggerin' quite a bit," Will said. "I'm guessin' he didn't make it very far. You can see drops of blood, too. If he headed north, I imagine we'll find him bled out before we cover much ground."

"Just ahead must be where he left his horse," Jonas said. "The ground's pretty well trampled. That pile of horse droppings ain't more'n a few hours old, neither."

"And he headed north, all right. You can see where he pushed his horse through the scrub. He might've turned off the trail, but I doubt it. Nowhere between here and Forth Worth to get help, that I know of, except mebbe an isolated ranch or farm. Let's get saddled up and take after him."

They had gone only about four miles when Will spotted buzzards circling in the clear blue sky.

"You want to bet that's not our horse thief those winged scavengers have found, pardner?"

Jonas shook his head.

"Not a chance. His tracks have been wandering all over the place for the last quarter-mile. Either he's not controlling his horse, or the animal's plumb worn out. Either way, I'd say it's the end of the trail for that bushwhackin' son of a bitch. Let's find out."

When they rounded the next bend, several of the buzzards had landed, and were feeding on a corpse. Will pulled out his rifle and fired a shot. The ungainly birds rose into the air, squawking in protest at having their gruesome meal interrupted.

"You reckon that's him?" Jonas said, when they rode up to the body and dismounted.

"We should know in a minute," Will answered. "He hasn't been here for much time. The buzzards haven't been chompin' on him all that long."

Will rolled the dead man onto his back.

"I don't recognize him, but this is the *hombre* you took a pot shot at, all right. You got him in the side, then the slug angled between his ribs and came out his belly. Must've torn up his guts somethin' fierce. I'm surprised he got as far as he did."

A weak whicker caught their attention. An emaciated sorrel mare, caked with dried sweat, dried blood from being gouged with spurs covering her flanks, emerged from a bosque of mesquite. She shuffled over to join Pete and Rebel, her head hanging. She half-heartedly nibbled at the grass.

"I reckon that must be the dead *hombre*'s horse," Will said. "He must've ridden her almost into the ground. No wonder he was tryin' to steal one of ours."

"Poor critter," Jonas said. "Now I *really* don't feel bad about pluggin' that son of a bitch. Any man who'd treat a horse like that needs killin'."

"I've gotta go along with you," Will said. "Let's check the saddlebags. There might be somethin' in 'em that'll tell us who her rider was. Then, I'm gonna brush her down some before we head out."

The mare stood calmly while Will and Jonas walked up to her. Will spoke softly to her, running his hand over her shoulder to reassure her. He tugged on the left saddlebag's straps and lifted the cover.

"Well, lookee here," he said, as he removed a canvas sack.

"What've you got, Will?" Jonas asked.

"A United States Mail bag. Says so right on it. Let's see what it holds."

Will opened the sack. The first thing he removed was a bundle of wrapped one-hundred-dollar federal bank notes.

Jonas whistled when he saw the money.

"I guess we know why he was in such an all-fired hurry. Must've held up a stage or a train. I'd wager he had a posse on his trail."

Will removed more bundles and stacked them on the ground.

"Twenty-five bills in each bundle, and twenty bundles. That makes a nice haul."

"Fifty thousand dollars' worth. That explains why he was ridin' so hard he damn near killed his horse. Wonder if there'll be a posse ridin' up on us soon."

"I doubt it," Will said. "He probably gave 'em the slip. If he hadn't, they most likely would have been here by now. The shape his horse is in also tells me they weren't close behind. She couldn't have been movin' at more'n a walk for several miles."

"Yeah, if he'd had to push her much farther, she would have collapsed right out from under him," Jonas said.

"I'll be just as happy if they don't catch up to us," Will said. "With this much money, whoever's after that *hombre*'ll be likely to shoot first, then ask questions later. They'd probably gun us down without givin' us the chance to explain we're Rangers."

"What're we gonna do with that *dinero*, and our thievin' dead friend?"

"We'll turn the money in to the Tarrant County sheriff, once we reach Fort Worth. I was gonna leave that *hombre* for the buzzards and coyotes, but we'd better bundle him up and take him along. Mebbe there's a wanted poster out on him. That'll slow us up some, but we've still got enough time to spare to make our train. Might as well get that chore done. Breakfast will have to be hardtack and water this mornin'."

"Long as we can get a good meal in Fort Worth, that's fine with me," Jonas said. "Let's break camp."

Will and Jonas's first stop in Fort Worth was the Tarrant County Sheriff's Office. A middle-aged deputy at the front desk looked up when they went inside.

"Afternoon, fellers," he said. "Anythin' in particular I can help you with?"

"Yep," Will answered. "Texas Rangers. My handle's Will Kirkpatrick. My pardner's is Jonas Peterson. We've got a dead *hombre* tied over his horse outside. He was carryin' this."

Will tossed the mail bag on the deputy's desk.

"There's fifty thousand dollars in there. All brand new hundred-dollar federal bank notes."

"Whew! Boy howdy. I reckon y'all had better speak to the Sheriff. I'll get him for you."

The deputy went through a door behind his desk. He returned a moment later with a burly man in his late forties, wearing a sheriff's star on his denim vest. He had sandy hair, a beard to match, and light brown eyes.

"Howdy, men. I'm Sheriff Abraham Newton. My deputy says you've brought in a body, and a mail sack full of cash."

"Ranger Will Kirkpatrick, and my pardner, Jonas Peterson. We sure did. The dead *hombre*'s tied over his horse, out front. You might want to have someone get him off the street before too many curious folks gather."

"That's not a bad idea. Tom, you and Scully take him down to Doc Xenelis."

"Right away, Sheriff."

"Doc Xenelis is the county coroner. He'll need to examine the deceased," Newton explained. "You mind tellin' me how you came up with this *hombre*?"

"Go ahead, Jonas," Will said.

"Okay. We were camped for the night, about twenty miles south. A slight noise must've woke me up. I noticed our horses were watching somethin' real suspicious-like. I followed their gaze, and spotted someone crawling through the brush. He was just about to untie the horses when I took a shot at him. I hit him, but he managed to reach his horse and get away. We found him this mornin', about four miles up the trail. He'd bled out."

"You didn't try'n warn him before you shot?" Newton asked.

"Nope. There wasn't time, plus I couldn't be sure he didn't have a pardner drawin' a bead on me. I wasn't takin' that chance."

"Understood."

Will picked up the narrative.

"When we came up on the *hombre*, the buzzards had just started workin' on him. His horse was just about played out, which explains why he was tryin' to steal one of ours. I found that mail sack in his saddlebags. Honestly, I first intended to leave him for the buzzards, seein' how he'd treated his animal, then tryin' to steal ours. But when I found that cash, I decided to tote him along and see if anyone recognized him, of if there's a wanted poster out for him."

"There just might be," Newton said. "What'd the man you brought in look like?"

"About average height and weight," Will answered. "About five eight- or nine, a hundred and seventy pounds. Has brown hair and eyes. Few days growth of whiskers, but a bushy moustache. About twenty-five years old. Wearing a gray shirt, butternut pants, and brown boots. Gray hat, green bandana. Was riding a sorrel mare, which he'd just about ridden into the ground."

"He sounds like the man we got a telegram on yesterday," Newton said. "Someone robbed the Katy Railroad Depot at Itasca about an hour before closing, just ahead of the southbound train's arrival. He clubbed the only passenger in the station over the head with his revolver, then held up the agent at gunpoint. The only things he took were the mailbags. The clerk tried to stop him, but took a bullet in the stomach for his efforts. He was able to describe the robber before he passed out. His description pretty much matches the dead man you boys toted in. He also shoved a young lady off her sorrel mare, and stole her horse. The Itasca marshal and his posse found the horse he'd been ridin' about ten miles out of town, along with one of the mailbags. He'd opened it and left the contents scattered on the ground. He kept the other one. That bag had a transfer of funds from a rancher outside town to the Cattlemen's Bank in Fort Worth."

"Seems funny the rancher sendin' the money didn't wait around to make certain it got on the train," Jonas said. "Also strange he knew about the shipment. Might've been an inside job."

"I thought the same thing at first, but then realized once the Katy's agent signed for it, the money became the railroad's responsibility. So the rancher wouldn't be out any money, but the railroad sure would've been. They'll be right glad you Rangers recovered it. And if it was an inside job, that'll be up to the railroad detectives to figure out."

"We'll have to make out a report," Will said. "That needs to be done right away, because we have a train to catch in a few hours. We'd like to have supper and get our horses fed before that."

"We can do that right now," Newton answered. "I don't suppose our man had any identification on him?"

"Not a shred," Will answered.

"Then until we can figure out who he was, if we ever do, we'll just write him up as a John

51

Doe. Soon as the report's done, we can take this cash over to the bank for safekeeping. Then you can take care of your other business. I'll find you if I need to."

"Can you make certain the girl's horse gets back to her?" Will asked. "She's in pretty tough shape, so she'll need a few days rest first."

"Of course. I'll be happy to. Tell you what. Once you get your horses taken care of, why don't I join you for supper? There's a cafe right next to the train depot that serves up decent grub. The prices are reasonable, too."

"That sounds like a good idea," Will agreed.

"Where you boys headed for?" Newton asked.

"Over past Sweetwater. There's some outlaw bunches stirrin' up trouble out that way. We're aimin' to stop 'em," Will said.

"Then you've got your work cut out for you, that's for damn sure," Newton said. He took some forms off a shelf.

"Sooner we fill these out, the sooner you can eat."

"Now you're talkin'," Jonas said.

4

"You just settle down, and take it easy," Will said to Pete, as he led his paint up the ramp and into the cattle car, which was attached to the back of a Texas and Pacific local. In addition to the old wood burning locomotive and tender, the train consisted of a mail and baggage car, two flat cars carrying rails and ties, a single passenger car, the horses' car, and a caboose.

"Same goes for you, Rebel," Jonas told his bay. "You don't need to be nervous. Be like Pete. Relax, and work on your hay. Your pal is already workin' on his."

Pete had indeed buried his muzzle in a pile of sweet-smelling hay. He was munching away while Will took the gear off him.

"Rebel'll be fine, once we get rollin'," Will assured Jonas. "Pete's ridden the train quite a bit, that's all. He's come to enjoy it."

"See, Rebel?" Jonas gave his horse a lump of sugar. "Nothin' to worry about. It's dang for certain gonna be easier on you than haulin' my butt two hundred miles across Texas."

Rebel whinnied, nipped at Jonas's ear, then grabbed a mouthful of hay and began chewing.

"That's better. I'll check on you at the next stop."

Jonas put his gear alongside Will's, in a corner of the car. He gave Rebel one last pat on the shoulder.

"You Rangers about ready?" the brakeman asked. "We're already a half-hour behind schedule. Got to try'n make up some lost time if we can."

"We are," Will answered. Once he and Jonas exited the car, the brakeman shoved the door shut, and latched it. Will and Jonas went to the passenger car. Most of the seats at the rear of the coach were already occupied. They settled into the third from the back pair of left-hand seats. The car was almost completely filled, its occupants a mixture of cowboys, drummers, and two young families.

The conductor shouted his "All aboard," then the train chuffed into motion.

"Might as well get some shut-eye," Will said. "Won't be anythin' to look at this time of the night anyway."

"I'm a mite worried about not bein' able to take the end seats," Jonas said, after he settled in the window seat. "Leaves our backs open."

"Same here, but there ain't nothin' we can do about it, unless we want to separate that family in 'em," Will answered. "I'm sure not hankerin' to do that."

He stretched out his legs, and tipped his hat over his eyes. Jonas followed suit. Lulled by the swaying motion of the train, and the clickety-clack of the wheels on the rails, both men were soon sound asleep.

Will was awakened by the first rays of the rising sun coming through his window, as the train rounded a curve. He nudged Jonas in the ribs with his elbow. Jonas snorted, and tipped back his hat.

"What'd ya go and wake me up for?" he muttered.

"Because the train's startin' to slow down. I'm not certain where we're at, but I sure hope we start makin' better time soon. I could have gone faster'n we did last night by ridin' Pete backwards all the way."

"We did seem to stop a lot," Jonas agreed. "And the engineer never did build up much steam."

The train had made several whistle-stops at small settlements to take on or discharge passengers, and two water stops. Even for a local, it was running considerably behind schedule.

"The locomotive seemed to have real trouble handling the grades, especially since there's not much to 'em, except a couple of cuts through the Palo Pinto Mountains," Will said. "Reckon I'll try'n hunt up the conductor, to see if he can tell us where the hell we're at. Our horses need water. They also need to get out and stretch their legs, if we've got a long enough stop."

Will started to get up. The front door of the car opened. The conductor came in, then stopped to make an announcement.

"We'll be making a water and wood stop in a few minutes. I apologize for all the delays. This will be our last stop before the town of Ranger. We're still about fifty miles from there. With any luck, there'll be another locomotive there, so we can switch out this one. It's got a problem with the boiler, which won't build up enough pressure for us to maintain full speed. We'll also change crews there. Once we reach the water stop, y'all will have time to get out and stretch your legs."

A man, who had boarded the train in the middle of the night, got up from his seat, which was right next to the conductor. He'd pulled a bandana over his face and tugged his hat low, so only his eyes were visible. He stuck his pistol in the conductor's ribs. At the same time, another man stood up in the rear of the car, covering the rest of the passengers with his six-gun.

"Don't anybody move, and nobody'll get hurt," the man in the front said. "My partner is going to take up a collection. Y'all are gonna donate all your valuables, cash, jewelry, gold money clips, whatever else we take a fancy to. Keep your hands where we can see 'em, and don't anyone make a move toward a gun. If anyone does, I'll put a bullet through this conductor, and my pard will put one through you. *Comprende?*"

He was answered with silence, and the passengers either raising their hands shoulder high or placing them on the backs of the seats.

"Good. As long as everyone cooperates, we'll leave you at the water stop. Now, start handin' over your valuables."

When the second bandit reached Will and Jonas, he ordered them to hand over their billfolds.

"I don't think so," Will said. "We're Texas Rangers. You're both under arrest." He kicked out with his right leg, catching the man in the side of his knee. Ligaments tore and the kneecap shattered at the impact. The man screamed and went down, dropping his gun. Will jumped on top of him, pinning him to the floor. His partner, shocked at the sudden turn of events, took his gun off the conductor, and fired one wild shot at Will, which missed, gouging a hole in the floor behind him. Jonas scrambled over Will and the still struggling bandit, yanking out his own gun and taking a snap shot at the first one, his bullet narrowly missing the man and punching a hole through the front door's window. Jonas ran up the aisle, dove to his belly, and slid at the bandit, knocking him off his feet. The man hit his head on the corner of a seat, stunning himself. Jonas covered him with his gun.

"Don't move," he ordered. "Will, you all right?" he called, as he rolled his man onto his belly and cuffed his hands behind his back.

Will also had his gun out and aimed at the second bandit.

"Yeah, I'm fine," he answered. "Everyone remain in your seats, and stay calm. We've got this here situation under control."

"You hurt, mister?" Jonas asked the conductor.

"No, just a bit shaky. I'm sure glad you Rangers took a hand. No tellin' what these *hombres* might have done otherwise. You want me to stop the train?"

"How far to the water stop?" Will asked.

"About half-a-mile."

"No, keep goin' until we reach it. I'm guessin' these *hombres* either have horses waitin' there, or partners. Which is it, mister?" he asked the bandit he held covered.

"Damn you. You busted my knee, and you want me to answer that? You can go to Hell, Ranger."

Will shoved the barrel of his Peacemaker deep into the man's gut, causing him to grunt.

"You don't answer my questions and you'll get there a lot faster'n I do."

"All right, all right. Just don't shoot me, Ranger, please. Me'n Burt planned this ourselves. We've got horses hidden in the brush behind the water tower."

"That's better. But we're gonna be ready, just in case you're lyin' and have a couple of friends waitin' in ambush. And *you'll* catch the first bullet if you are. That's a fact."

"I'm tellin' the truth, Ranger, honest."

"Is he, Burt?" Jonas asked the other robber.

"He is."

"He'd better be. Or you'll get the second bullet. What's your name, *hombre*?"

"Burt. Burt Pardee. My pard is Joel Gray."

Jonas pulled Gray to his feet, and walked him back to where Will was waiting. They sat the two men on the floor at the back of the car.

"Once the train stops, you keep an eye on these two buzzards while I make certain they don't have any friends waitin'," Will told Jonas. "While the engine's takin' on water and wood, I'll locate their horses. I'll put 'em in the car with ours. Conductor, it might take me a few minutes."

"It'll take us at least twenty to fill the boiler and load up the tender, Ranger. There's also a ramp and platform, which'll make loading those animals easier."

"What about my knee?" Gray whined.

"That's gonna have to wait until we reach Ranger, and find a doc," Will said. "After that, it's straight to the jail."

5

"We've got a couple of hours to kill," Will said, after he and Jonas dropped off their prisoners at the Ranger town jail. They had also left their horses in a corral at the livery stable, where they could eat, drink, and stretch their legs. "We might as well take the time to get a good meal."

"Sounds reasonable, but we're gonna die of old age before we ever get to Sweetwater," Jonas grumbled.

"Better'n dyin' with a bullet in your belly," Will answered, with a laugh. He pointed across the street, to a sign swaying in the breeze.

"Ma's Café. Good Down Home Cookin'," he read. "Sound like a decent place to try, pardner?" he asked.

Jonas shook his head.

"I dunno. My ma was a terrible cook."

"And mine never did make a meal. My family, long as I can remember, always had a full-time cook."

"Yeah, well, your family has just a tad more money than mine ever did," Jonas answered.

"I reckon that's so," Will conceded.

Will's father was a wealthy banker. He, along with Will's mother, had objected strenuously when Will joined the Rangers, instead of following his father into the family business. They'd only reconciled after Will and Jonas caught the men who robbed the family bank, trying to pin the crime on Will's father.

"Then we might as well try the place, Will. How bad could it be?"

"Let's hope we don't find out."

They walked across the dusty street and into the restaurant. There were only two other customers in the place. A twenty-something blonde, blue-eyed woman greeted them. The simple gingham dress she wore did nothing to hide the curves of her figure, the lace at its bodice merely emphasizing her buxom bosom.

"Howdy, boys. C'mon in. Take any table you'd like. I'll be with you in just a minute. You gonna want coffee?"

"We sure are. Bring the pot," Will answered.

"You've got it," the woman replied.

The two Rangers chose a table in the back corner of the small restaurant, where they could keep their backs to the wall and their gaze on the front door. The woman placed a plate of ham and eggs in front of one of the other customers, then walked over to their table. She put a pot of coffee and two mugs in the center of the table.

"Afternoon, boys," she said. "You must be new in town. I ain't seen you before."

"We're just passin' through on our way to

Sweetwater," Will answered. "Waitin' for our train to get rollin' again."

"Honey chile, if y'all are waitin' on that Texas and Pacific local, you'd be better off walkin'. That train ain't never on time."

"So we've noticed," Will said.

"Of course, I hear tell a pair of *malo hombres* tried to hold up the passengers. That made the train even later. Lucky a pair of Texas Rangers was on the train, and stopped 'em. You see that happen?"

"I'd imagine so," Will answered. "We're the Rangers."

"Boy howdy, if that don't beat all. Rangers here in Ranger. Sure hope you two ain't lookin' for the old Ranger encampment this here town's named for. It's long gone."

"No, we're not," Will said. "We're headed farther west."

"Beggin' your pardon, ma'am, but you sure don't look like a 'Ma' to me," Jonas said. "I know my own ma was nowhere near as purty as you."

"What? Oh, you mean the name on the sign out front. That was my grandma. When she passed, my ma took over. Now she's takin' life easy, and I run the place. But I *am* a mother. Got two little ones, a boy and a girl. They stay with my ma and pa while I work. I'd imagine you've already met the marshal. He's my husband. And if you don't mind my sayin' so, you sure don't look old enough to be a Ranger to me."

Jonas blushed.

"I am, but just barely."

"Dagnab it, Jonas, you sure keep puttin' your foot in it," Will said.

"It's all right. Just so long as you call me by my Christian name . . . Evelyn," the restaurant owner said.

"I promise," Jonas said. "My name's Jonas. My pard, here, is Will."

"Not that that's settled, what'll you boys have? I've got steak and spuds, or pork chops and spuds. Fried taters, pinto beans, and peach pie to top things off. Or ham and eggs, if you prefer."

"The pork chops sound good to me," Will said.

"Same here," said Jonas.

"Fine, two orders of hog and spuds, comin' right up."

"That was a dang fine meal," Jonas said, as he and Jonas stood on the boardwalk in front of the restaurant, smoking. "What do you want to do now? Get a couple of beers?"

"That's not a bad idea, but I reckon we'd better head on down to the depot and see how much longer until our train leaves. Mebbe we got lucky, and it didn't take 'em as long to switch out the engine and crew as they figured. We'll pick up our horses on the way."

• • •

The Rangers retrieved their horses from the livery, then made the short ride to the railroad station. The station agent was on the platform, waiting for them.

"You men have good timing," he said. "They've just finished up filling the tender with wood. The train'll be backing up to the platform in just a few minutes. Soon as it does, you can load your horses and reboard."

"Was fresh hay and water put in the car for our horses?" Will asked.

"They sure were, Ranger. I know how important those horses are to you, so I made certain of it."

"*Gracias*. We're much obliged."

Half-an-hour later, their horses loaded, and Will and Jonas climbed back into the passenger coach.

"All aboard!" the conductor shouted. "Next station, Eastland."

"Will, you happen to have a funny feelin' about this train?" Jonas asked under his breath, when the train rolled out of Ranger.

"Why? Somethin' botherin' you?"

"Yeah. The way this whole trip's been goin' just sticks in my craw."

"How so?"

"Lots of little things that just don't add up. Why all the delays? Even for a local pulled by an old locomotive like this one, there's been an awful lot of unexplained delays."

"Trains break down, or rails get bent all the time," Will answered, with a shrug. "A herd of cattle or buffalo wanderin' across the tracks will hold up a train, sometimes for hours."

"Not so many times in such a short stretch. Then those two *hombres* that tried to rob it. Didn't seem too smart, tryin' to rob a train with only a few passengers in one car. Wouldn't have been enough money for those sons of bitches to buy a decent bottle of red-eye. Unless they had bigger fish to fry. I dunno, maybe I'm worried about nothin', but I've just got a feelin' deep in my gut that something else bad's about to happen before we get to Sweetwater."

"I've seen too many hunches play out not to listen to yours," Will said. "We'll just have to be ready if anything does happen."

"There's two more things," Jonas said. "First, the conductor didn't seem all that upset when those two *hombres* attempted their robbery. If I didn't know better, I'd say it bothered him more that we stopped it."

"You never know how someone will react in a situation like that," Will pointed out. "What else?"

"Yeah. Why didn't the conductor change out with the rest of the crew back in Ranger? Also, the express car. There's been no mail taken on or dropped off anywhere we've stopped. No sign of a messenger, either. That just seems mighty strange."

"I hadn't thought about it, but you're right about both. You've got good instincts, Jonas. I'm glad you're now on the law's side, rather'n headin' down your kinfolks' path. You would have been one tough *hombre* for the law to deal with. Well, all we can do for now is watch and wait. Mebbe your hunch will turn out to be nothing. Could be the conductor's replacement got sick, and there just wasn't any mail for this trip. With luck, nothin' else will happen."

"I sure hope so, but the knot in my belly is tellin' me otherwise," Jonas said.

The train made a brief stop in Eastland to take on and discharge passengers, the resumed its westbound trip. It was about two miles out of Cisco, rounding a curve, when Jonas looked out the window.

"There seems to be somethin' on the tracks," he said, just as the train's whistle gave a long, loud blast. The engineer pulled back hard on the brakes. Metal on metal screamed and sparks flew when the wheels locked up and the train shuddered to a halt.

Jonas got a closer look.

"Will, that's someone layin' across the rails. Hold on, he's gettin' up. He's headin' for the engine, with a gun in his hand. Looks like another one comin' out of the brush."

"Which means your hunch is definitely right," Will said. "They've gotta be part of another robbery attempt. We've got to stop 'em. Let's get movin'."

To the passengers, he ordered, "Everyone stay in your seats. Don't leave this car. You'll be takin' a chance on gettin' shot if you do."

Will and Jonas drew their pistols and jumped out of the car. The train was already moving as soon as their boots hit the ground. They lunged for the steps on the rearmost flat car, scrambling up onto its load of ties as the train gathered speed.

"Stay low," Will ordered. "Let's hope they don't look back. With luck, they'll be too busy dealin' with the engineer and fireman."

"I'm hopin' the doors on the mail car ain't locked," Jonas answered. "I'm sure not lookin' forward to havin' to climb over its roof. We'll be sittin' ducks if those *hombres* spot us."

The train began to pick up speed as Will and Jonas worked their way over the flat cars. When they reached the express car, Will spread his legs wide to balance against the rocking of the train, while he shoved hard against the express car door. It refused to budge.

"Damn, Jonas. It's locked. We'll have to go over the top. Keep low until we get close to the engine."

Jonas nodded his assent.

They climbed the ladder to the roof, dropping

to their hands and knees to crawl toward the engine. The wind blew their hats off, only the chinstraps keeping them on the backs of their necks. Smoke and cinders from the locomotive stung their skin and burned their eyes. Fighting for every handhold, they made it to the front of the car.

"Both of 'em are in the cab," Will said. "One of 'em's got his gun on the engineer, the other on the fireman. At least they haven't spotted us yet."

"You want to try'n pick 'em off from here?" Jonas asked.

Will shook his head.

"It's too risky. We can't get a clean shot with the train rockin' and rollin'. We'd be just as likely to hit one of the trainmen as the robbers."

"What're we gonna do?"

"I'm gonna drop down into the tender, then work my way to the cab."

"You'll get killed before you make it halfway," Jonas protested.

"No, unless one of those sons of bitches makes a lucky shot," Will answered. "That's where you come in. You're gonna cover me. As soon as one of those *hombres* spots me, you start slingin' lead around the cab. That'll make 'em duck, which will give me time to jump 'em."

"I've only got my six-gun. Odds are one of those bastards will plug you while I'm reloading," Jonas said.

"Not likely." Will shook his head again. "They'll have as much trouble getting a clean shot as we will. Plus, I can duck behind the wood for cover. Our biggest worry is a ricochet takin' out the engineer or fireman. Let's get this done before one of 'em looks back. You ready?"

Jonas nodded.

"Good. Here goes."

Will jumped into the tender. He stumbled when he hit the woodpile, and fell headlong, dropping his gun into the lengths of wood. One of the bandits heard him. He turned and fired a quick shot, which split the air over Will's head. From the roof of the express car, flat on his belly, Jonas quickly fired six bullets into the locomotive's cab, driving the man back. He hurriedly reloaded, and resumed shooting.

The fireman, seeing the outlaw covering him distracted, swung his shovel at the man's legs, cutting them out from under him. The outlaw toppled against the firebox, screaming in pain as the red-hot metal sizzled his flesh.

Will retrieved his pistol, and put a bullet into the back of the man covering the engineer. Once the man went down, the engineer pulled back hard on the brake lever. The train's sudden stop jarred Jonas from his perch. He flew off the express car's roof, flipped in mid-air, then crashed into Will before landing on his back, on top of the woodpile. He gasped for air.

"You all right, Jonas?" Will asked.

"Yeah, seem to be. Thanks for breakin' my fall. I'm obliged."

"Wasn't part of the plan," Will answered, with a chuckle. "Let's check on those *hombres* in the cab."

He and Jonas climbed out of the tender and into the locomotive.

"Texas Rangers," Will said. "You men all right?"

"We are now, thanks to you two," the fireman said. "Where the hell'd you come from?"

"We've been on this train since Fort Worth," Will answered. "One of you go back and tell the conductor to keep all the passengers inside. Him, too. Then get right back here."

"I'll take care of it," the fireman said.

Will checked the man he'd shot, who was dead, then hunkered on his heels alongside the wounded bandit.

"All right, mister. This is the second attempted robbery of this train. I can't figure out why in the blue blazes anyone would attempt to rob a local, that has only one passenger car, unless there's somethin' I ain't been told. But you're gonna tell me."

"I . . . need a doctor. My leg's busted . . . And it feels like half my skin's been . . . burned off."

"I'll get you a doc, soon as you tell me what I want to know."

The man shook his head.

"I can't."

Will placed the barrel of his Peacemaker against the bridge of the man's nose.

"Let me put it to you another way. Your pard's dead. The other two men who tried to rob this train are behind bars, back in Ranger. So, I can either get you to a doctor, or I can put you out of your misery with one quick bullet, and send you straight to Hell along with your *compadre*. Which'll it be?"

When the man hesitated, Will cocked the hammer of his pistol. The man's eyes widened in terror at the ominous click.

"I . . . I just can't."

"Your decision."

Will eased back the trigger.

"No. No! Don't pull that trigger. I'll talk."

"I thought you might."

Will uncocked the gun, but kept it pressed against the man's forehead.

"Start."

"There's two hundred thousand dollars in brand new gold double eagles bein' shipped from the Philadelphia mint to the El Paso National Bank in the mail car."

"That doesn't make any sense," Jonas said. "There's no sign of a guard on this train, plus with so many stops, there's a lot more places where it could be held up."

"The Treasury Department and railroad put out the word that the *dinero* was on the Shreveport Limited. Put some decoy strong boxes on that train, and a lot of guards to make it look real. But the Limited's a decoy. The gold is on this train. No one'd suspect a slow train like this one would be carrying a fortune."

"So you and your pardner tried to get it for yourselves," Will said. He turned to the engineer.

"Did you know anythin' about this?"

"No. No, sir, Ranger. No idea."

"Well, word sure got out somehow," Will said. "What else do you know?"

"The other two men were supposed to hold the passengers hostage until we got the gold off the train. You Rangers threw a monkey wrench into our plans."

"The fireman's comin' back, Will," Jonas said.

"Good. Soon as he gets some steam built back up we'll get movin'. Guess we'll be in Cisco a mite longer than we planned."

"We can't continue to Cisco, Ranger," the engineer said.

"Why not?"

"Because unless this *hombre* is a bigger liar than I figure, he said he's part of a gang that's got the tracks blocked at the T & P's intersection with the Houston and Texas Central. We'll have to back up to Eastland."

"He tellin' me the truth, mister?"

"Yeah, Ranger, he is. I was gonna tell you, honest. Me and my partners' jobs were to take control of this train, then make certain it stopped at the blockade, without any trouble. There's a cattle car with ten men in it, that was rolled across the tracks. They'll kill anyone who tries to stop us."

The fireman climbed back into the cab.

"You got everything settled with the passengers?" Will asked.

"Yeah. Something's strange, though."

"What do you mean?"

"Max, he's the conductor, got mighty quiet when I told him what had happened. Didn't look happy at all."

"He's probably the inside man, like you suspected, Jonas," Will said.

"He's most likely not the only one," Will answered.

He thumbed back his Stetson.

"You said there's only a cattle car blocking the rails?" he asked the robber.

"Yeah, Just an old one. We picked it because it'll be easy to defend, against this train and townsfolk alike. Plenty of slots to fire from, and not much cover around the junction."

Jonas rubbed his jaw, then spoke up.

"Will, it's a long shot, but mebbe, just mebbe, we could ram our way through that blockade."

"Jonas, that'd be plumb loco."

"No, Ranger, it might not be," the engineer said. "Charlie, do you think you could build up enough steam to get us goin' about thirty miles an hour before we reach Cisco?"

"It'd take some doin', but yeah. I could manage it, Joe."

"Wouldn't this thing jump the tracks?" Will asked.

"Might, might not," the engineer answered. "But I've been drivin' trains for nigh onto thirty years now. This here Ol' Number 10 might not look like much, but she's one almighty tough gal. If we hit that old car at just the right speed, we'll cut clean through that damn thing just like a hot knife through butter. If any of the *hombres* inside it are still movin' after that, it'll be real easy to clean up what's left of 'em."

"We could go back to Eastland, and get help there. Send a wire ahead to Cisco from the station, askin' for more help," Will said.

"We could, but that'd take too much time," Jonas said. "Those *hombres* might figure out somethin's gone wrong and take off. Or, decide to hit the town instead."

"I'm just tryin' to think this through," Will answered. "I'd hate to see any of the passengers get hurt."

"Most likely, a few folks are gonna get hurt no matter how we play this," Jonas answered.

"I know." Will sighed. "And ramming that

car *will* take those renegades by surprise. Engineer . . ."

"Joe. My fireman's Charlie."

"Joe, are you certain my pardner's idea will work?"

"I'd say about eight in ten. I can't give better odds than that."

"Then let's try it. Charlie, start chuckin' wood. Joe, hit the throttle. Just remember, when those *hombres* blocking the tracks start shootin', Joe, keep your head inside. We can't chance one of 'em pickin' you off."

Charlie opened the firebox door and started tossing chunks of wood onto the flames. While the train picked up speed, Will and Jonas reloaded their guns. They each took a spot at the cab's side windows.

"There's a slight left-hand curve just before we reach the crossing," Joe said, shouting to be heard above the noise of the locomotive and rush of the wind. "As soon as we round that, we'll be in sight of the blockade. It'll be less than a quarter-mile ahead of us. Soon as we reach the spot, I'll duck down, but keep my hand on the throttle. That'll leave you the whole window for yourself, Ranger. Give you a chance for some better shots."

Will merely nodded his understanding.

The train kept gathering speed as it neared Cisco. When it rounded the bend, and the cattle car blocking the tracks came into sight, Joe grabbed the chain for the whistle, letting out a long blast as he bent low, the throttle still pulled back to full speed.

The waiting robbers saw the onrushing train. Rifles were poked between the slats of the cattle car. Bullets began raking the engine, pinging off its boiler jacket and ricocheting wildly. In the cab, Will and Jonas fired back, knowing their pistols were of little use under the circumstances. All they could do was force an outlaw or two to duck, if one of their bullets actually made a hit near him.

The train robbers had no time to jump from their car as the local bore down on it. At almost twenty-five miles per hour, the locomotive sliced through the dried out wood of the cattle car. Shattered pieces of car flew in every direction. Joe shoved the throttle forward to the stop position, pulled back on the Johnson bar to put the engine into reverse, and jammed the brake lever into full stop. Metal screeched and sparks flew as the train, wheels locked, slid to a stop a hundred yards beyond the demolished blockade.

"You two all right?" Will asked the fireman and engineer. "Can you keep an eye on this *hombre*?"

"We sure can," Joe answered.

"Good. We're goin' to see what's left of those renegades."

Will and Jonas jumped out of the engine. The

conductor was just exiting the passenger coach when they reached it.

"What the hell is goin' on?" he asked.

"Robbery. No time to explain more," Will answered. "Don't let the passengers outta that car, until we say so. I'd imagine some folks are already on their way from town to lend a hand. They can tend to anyone's hurts."

Ten men were sprawled in and around the wreckage of the cattle car. Six of them were already dead, two more had injuries so severe it was doubtful they would last the night. Two more had serious, but not life threatening, injuries. One of those tried to lift and aim his gun at Will, who easily took it from the man's grasp.

"You're damn lucky you're still alive," Will said. "Don't push your luck."

"You find anyone else alive, Will?" Jonas called.

"Nope. Just this one, and the other three."

"Looks like the town marshal comin'," Jonas said, indicating a pudgy man wearing a badge on his cowhide vest. "The conductor's with him. So's the doc."

The three men walked up to the Rangers. The doctor nodded, then went to treat the survivors.

"You mind explaining what the devil all this is about, mister?" the marshal asked.

"Best as I can," Will said. "I'm Texas Ranger

Will Kirkpatrick. This here's my ridin' pardner, Jonas Peterson. We're headed for Sweetwater. This was an attempted train robbery. We stopped it."

"And made one helluva mess," the marshal said. "But the town appreciates what you did. Those *hombres* had me and my deputy pinned down. None of the townsfolk wanted to take a hand. Not that I blame 'em. Why get killed for the railroad's sake? Name's Jep Hanratty, by the way."

"What happened to your deputy?"

"He's helpin' people on the train. Nobody's hurt bad, just some bumps and bruises, maybe one broken leg. We'll take everyone to the hotel until this is settled."

"*Bueno.*"

Will gave the conductor a sharp look.

"What I'd like to know is how these men knew when the train would reach Cisco, especially since it's runnin' so late. Would you care to explain that, Mister . . ."

"Sloan. Maxwell Sloan."

"I'm waitin'," Will snapped.

"I'm not just the conductor," Sloan said. "I'm also a Pinkerton agent."

Jonas shook his head.

"A Pinkerton. Figures they'd be involved somehow."

"Let him talk," Will said.

"We knew there was a plan to rob the Treasury shipment," Sloan said. "We even knew who the inside man was. We just didn't know where, or how, it would happen. So we had to wait until the gang made their move. Now I can wire back to Fort Worth, and have the leader of the outfit arrested."

"You happen to have any identification?" Will asked.

"Certainly."

"Take it out. Easy."

Will kept his gun aimed at Sloan, who removed his papers from his inside vest pocket. He handed them to Will.

"These seem in order," Will said. He passed them back to Sloan.

"Marshal, how strong is the vault in your town's bank?" Will asked.

"About as good as any small town's bank," Hanratty answered.

"In other words, not much good at all," Will said.

"Right, Ranger. Why are you askin'?"

"Because this train's carryin' two hundred thousand dollars in new gold coins," Will answered. "We need to make certain no other renegades try for it."

"Who told you that, Ranger?" Sloan asked.

"The outlaw on the locomotive . . . the one that's still alive."

79

"Well, he's wrong," Sloan said. "That money's on the original train. This one was a decoy."

"What?"

"We knew the inside man would tell his men which train the money was actually on. So, we pulled a double switch. Orders were cut showing this train would carry the shipment. But it was moved back to the original train. You don't think there's any way the Texas and Pacific would have allowed a fortune in gold coins like that to be put on a clunker like this? The only thing in those strongboxes is rocks."

"Mr. Sloan, let me get this straight. You, and the railroad, placed the lives of innocent people in danger, knowing full well a gang of outlaws would attack an unguarded train. And that most likely, people would have been killed, if we hadn't just by coincidence been on this run. Also, how did you expect the gang wouldn't know who you were, and gun you down?"

"The two men you shot and jailed back in Ranger were also Pinkertons," Sloan said. "We'd worked our way into the gang. Of course, they, nor I, couldn't reveal that, without revealing our modus operandi. When you Rangers interfered, you really made a mess of things."

"Did it ever occur to you someone else might have taken a hand?"

"If they had, we would have neutralized them," Sloan said, with a shrug.

"You mean killed them, don't you?"

"If it became necessary, yes. A small price to pay to save the United States Government a tidy sum of money."

Will spat in the dust between Sloan's feet.

"You mean the Texas and Pacific, since once they received the shipment, it was their responsibility."

"Well, yes. The railroad *is* our client. A very valuable client."

"Sloan, you make me sick," Will said. "In fact, the entire Pinkerton organization makes me sick. Most of you are thugs, working for the rich, while keeping the working man down in the dirt."

"I really don't care what you think of me, Ranger," Sloan answered.

"Jonas, Marshal, let's get to work cleanin' this mess up, and getting the men still alive in jail. We need to check on our horses, too. Have to make certain they didn't get hurt in the wreck. Before I do somethin' I really shouldn't do."

He turned away from Sloan.

"Aw, the hell with it."

Will turned back, and slugged the Pinkerton right on the point of his chin, snapping his neck back. Sloan dropped to the ground, out cold.

"Damn, that felt good."

"Ranger, he's gonna make trouble when he comes to," Hanratty said.

"How? Did you see me hit him?"

"Um, no sir, Ranger. I don't know what happened to him. He must've tripped over something and hit his head. Yeah, that's it."

"Did you see anythin', Jonas?"

Jonas shook his head.

"I didn't see a thing, Will. I was too busy tryin' to get this wounded man to his feet."

"See, Marshal. There's no problem at all."

Will and Jonas were in Marshal Hanratty's office. The train had been moved to the depot, where the Rangers removed their horses, and took them to the local livery stable. The dead outlaws' bodies were at the hardware store, which doubled as the funeral parlor. The three most seriously injured men, including the one from the engine, were at the doctor's office, the other two in cells.

The office door opened. Maxwell Sloan stepped inside, trailed by Bob Tucker, Hanratty's deputy. Sloan had a bandage wrapped around his jaw, tied at the nape of his neck.

"Marshal, I wanted that man arrested for assault!" Sloan shouted. "Attempted murder, if you think you can make it stick."

"You win the bet, Ranger," Hanratty said. "His jaw ain't broke. I figured for certain it was."

He shook his head, and slid two silver dollars across his desk to Jonas.

"I knew it wasn't," Jonas answered, as he

picked up the coins. "If my pard really wanted to bust this *hombre*'s jaw, it'd be busted."

"Marshal, are you listening to me?" Sloan asked. "I said I want that man arrested."

"Now, hold on just one minute, Mister Sloan," Hanratty said. He held out his hands, palms forward, in a calming gesture. "Do you have any proof of your accusation?"

"You were all there," Sloan said. "You saw him hit me. All of you did."

"I didn't see any such thing," Hanrattty answered. "Neither did my deputy. Right, Bob?"

"Ranger Kirkpatrick hit an innocent man? No, I sure did not," Tucker said.

"I don't suppose there's any use asking you if you saw your partner hit me?" Sloan asked Jonas.

"You can ask, but I didn't see anything like that," Jonas answered. "All I saw when I turned around was you on the ground, unconscious."

"You won't get away with this. I'll have Mr. Pinkerton contact the governor!" Sloan shouted.

"Before you do, you might want to hear this," Will answered. "I'm placing you under arrest for reckless endangerment. You put the lives of every passenger on that train, and the crew, in jeopardy. You had no right to put an unguarded Treasury shipment on a train full of civilians."

"I had every right," Sloan said.

"Hold on. There's more. You're also under

arrest for attempted train robbery, destruction of railroad property, and suspicion of murder. Also, once the United States Marshal arrives, you'll be charged with stealing a United States Treasury shipment."

"Where the hell did you come up with that, Ranger? You've got no evidence. I'm in charge of *protecting* the shipment."

"You were protecting it. For yourself. Your man in the locomotive's cab talked. Seems he wanted to be prepared to meet his Maker, since he might not live. *You're* the inside man. The conductor who was supposed to take over for you in Ranger was found murdered. What, did you honestly think I wouldn't check your story?"

"I didn't think you'd see any reason to."

"Then you're not as smart as I thought."

"Why would I do all those things, which I didn't, for a bunch of rocks?"

"Because the strongboxes on this train are loaded with gold coins, not rocks. You pulled a triple switch, Sloan. Just like a con man with a shell game, hidin' the pea so the victims never win. I figure you also told the Houston and Texas Central to block the tracks. You would've had to make certain another train wasn't comin' through, until you'd completed your scheme. I have to admit, it was right clever."

"How would you know that, Ranger? No one has the keys for the locks. Not even me."

Will eased his Peacemaker out of his holster and pointed it at the Pinkerton's stomach.

"Mr. Sam Colt can open any lock."

"With a little help from Mr. Crow-Bar," Jonas said, picking up a pry bar from the table next to him.

Marshal Hanratty was now holding a shotgun.

"Mister Remington lent a hand, too."

"So did Misters Smith and Wesson," Tucker added. He had also pulled his gun, and jabbed the American's barrel into Sloan's back.

"There's a nice cell waiting for you through that door," the deputy continued. "You want to get movin'? I purely hate the idea of havin' to clean pieces of backbone, guts, and blood off the floor if you make me shoot you."

Will stood up.

"I'd take his advice. Otherwise, I might just have to shoot you from the front."

Sloan lifted his hands shoulder high.

"All right, Ranger. I'll play along with your little game. But there's no way you can make those charges stick. You've got no real evidence. All you have is hunches, and the words of a dying man. As soon as I can wire Allan Pinkerton, he'll arrange for my bail. He's also got the best attorneys in the country at his disposal. I'll be set free before the week is out."

"The telegraph office is closed," Hanratty said. "You'll be able to send a message to your boss as soon as it opens in the morning. For now, head for that cell. Two of your men are in the one next to it. I'll have supper brought to you in a bit."

Tucker escorted the Pinkerton to his cell. When he returned, he closed the heavy oak door separating the cells from the office. He placed two short-barreled pistols and a knife on Hanratty's desk.

"I see you had to defang the sidewinder," the marshal said.

"I sure did. He didn't give me any trouble. He's locked up nice and tight."

"Which is kind of surprising," Jonas noted. "He knows he's trapped."

"I wouldn't be so certain, son," Hanratty said. "He's gotta be smart enough to realize the evidence is pretty flimsy. Yeah, you and your pardner have it, but proving it's another story."

"Jep's right," Will said. "That's why we've got more work to do. We need to make certain our case is air tight. I'm kind of surprised our detective friend hasn't figured out I'm runnin' a bluff."

"He just might have, and doesn't want to tip his hand," Hanratty said. "He's probably still tryin' to figure out a way to keep his hands on all that *dinero*."

"Jep, I'm getting' kinda hungry," Tucker said. "You mind if I wander over to the café to get some chuck?"

"No, Bob. Go right ahead. I'll eat later."

"How about you fellers?" he asked Will and Jonas.

"My belly says it could stand a bite," Jonas said. "That all right, Will?"

"Sure. Take your time. I'll eat with the marshal."

"Bob, have Monica make up plates for the prisoners."

"Will do."

Jonas stood up, and crossed the room. Just as Tucker opened the front door, a tremendous explosion rocked the building. Jonas was blown into the street. The door to the cells, blown out of its frame, landed on top of Tucker. Will was knocked out of his chair as the roof lifted off, then crashed down, burying him and the two local officers under a mound of debris. The entire scene was enveloped by a thick cloud of smoke and dust.

6

Will blacked out for a few moments. When he came to, he heard Jonas calling his name. His partner sounded as if he were a mile away.

Will attempted to answer, but his mouth and nose were clogged with dirt and dust, so much so that he could barely breathe. He was lying on his right side, with his arm pinned underneath. His left arm and hand were still free, in a small air pocket above him. He pounded and scratched at the debris trapping him. He paused for a moment. He heard nothing, so he started knocking again. This time, he got a response. It was Jonas.

"Will? You under there?"

Will pounded as hard as he could.

"All right, Will. I hear you. Don't try'n dig yourself out. The pile over you is mighty unstable. You make one wrong move and it's liable to collapse on top of you. You understand? Knock once if you do."

Will knocked once.

"All right. Don't go anywhere. I'll get some help. We'll have you out of there in a jiffy."

Silence again descended on the black pit entombing Will. He was soaked with sweat. Breathing was difficult, with oxygen limited in the small space. It seemed an eternity before Jonas returned.

"Will, you still with us?"

Will knocked.

"Good. Hang on, pard, I've got some help."

Will heard men pulling up pieces of wood, chunks of brick and adobe, other debris, and tossing them aside. After about fifteen minutes, a narrow beam of light came through an opening above him. He slapped his hand against a board.

"I hear you, Will," Jonas shouted. "I can see your hat, too. It'll only be a few more minutes."

The opening was swiftly enlarged. Once Will's head and shoulders were free, Jonas reached down, slid his hands under Will's shoulders, and attempted to pull him loose. When he did, the debris pile shifted. Will hollered in pain when a beam dropped across his legs.

"Sorry, Will," Jonas said. "Guess we've gotta do some more diggin'."

The men resumed their work. Soon, Will's entire upper body was freed. His legs were still pinned by the heavy oak beam.

"Will, we've got to find a thick board, to use as a lever to get your legs free," Jonas said.

"You'd better hurry," Will answered, gritting his teeth against the pain. "They're starting to go numb."

"Be quick as we can."

In less than five minutes, Jonas returned. He and several other men gingerly maneuvered a long plank under the beam trapping Will.

"Be ready, as soon as that beam is lifted, Will," Jonas said. "We won't be able to hold it long. Soon as it shifts, I'll pull you out from under it."

Will nodded.

"Let's go," Jonas said.

The only person Will could now see from his prison was Jonas. He knew it would take several men to put enough pressure on the makeshift lever to move the beam sufficiently to break him loose. The beam began to creak as it shifted ever so slightly.

"Any luck yet?" Jonas shouted.

"I think it's startin' to give," Will answered. "I can wriggle a couple of inches."

"Push down harder, boys," Jonas ordered. With a groan, the beam lifted about four inches.

"You've got it," Will yelled.

Jonas left the beam to the others. He grabbed Will and pulled him back, up and out from under the jumble of wood, bricks, adobe, and smashed furniture. The other men, at the end of their strength, let the beam crash back down.

As soon as he was free, Will attempted to stand up, but his knees buckled. He sat on an overturned bookcase.

"You'd better take it easy a few minutes, pard," Jonas said. "You might have a busted leg, or some torn muscles."

Will shook his head.

"I don't think so. Just need a couple of minutes to get the blood circulatin' again, so I have feeling back in my legs. You all right?"

"Yup. Just got some bumps when I landed in the street."

"What about the marshal and deputy?"

"The marshal has a few cuts, maybe a busted arm. He got lucky. He ended up under his desk. That protected him from the rest of the stuff that came down on him. The doc's with him now. There's some men still tryin' to dig the deputy out. Dunno what kind of shape he's in."

"Anybody checked on our prisoners?"

"Not yet. We've been too busy tryin' to get you and the other men out before y'all suffocated. I doubt any of 'em are still alive. The explosion came from back in the cells."

"Damn! They might have escaped."

"That'd be pretty much impossible. There's not much left back there."

"We're gonna make certain of that, Jonas. Right now. Get a couple of men to help us."

Jonas gestured to two of the men who had just helped him free Will.

"Eli, Malachi, come with us. We've got to see if we can find anything of the prisoners."

"The only thing we'll find is a few bits of skin and bone," Malachi said.

"If that," Eli added.

"I've just got to make certain they died in

the explosion, or if they somehow managed to escape," Will answered.

"You sayin' someone got them out of there, then blew up the jail?" Eli asked.

"I doubt it. We would have heard something," Will answered. "But I've got to be sure."

Most of the wall separating the cells from the office had crumbled. However, the thick stone exterior walls of the building had withstood the explosion virtually unscathed. The twisted remains of the cell bars protruded at odd angles from the mounds of rubble covering the floor.

"Let's start digging," Will ordered. "You two men start with what's left of the first cell. Me'n Jonas'll see if we can find the *hombre* in the other. I've got a gut feelin' he's the man that blew up the jail. One thing's for certain. The explosion was in his cell. There's a hollow in the pile of rubble in that one. Most likely there's a crater under it."

"All right," Malachi said.

They began digging with their bare hands, picking up pieces of debris and tossing them aside. Malachi and Eli found the first body, which was crushed almost beyond recognition.

"Ranger, we've found one," Eli called.

"I'll be right there," Will answered. "Jonas, you keep digging."

Jonas nodded.

Will examined the body, able to place its badly

smashed face as one of the train robbers. He returned to where Jonas was still working, and started to lift a larger piece of roof.

"You want a hand, Will?" Jonas asked.

"I could use one."

"Be right there."

Jonas crossed the small space, and passed a bloody object to Will. Will started to take it, then gagged, and dropped it.

"What the hell is that?"

"It's a hand. I asked if you wanted one." Jonas said, with a soft chuckle. "There's more body parts in the corner. I found 'em under a mattress."

"You're one sick *hombre*. Show 'em to me."

Jonas took Will to the far back corner of Sloan's cell.

"You might want to get ready to puke your guts out," Jonas warned him. He turned over the burnt, tattered remains of a mattress. Underneath was what was left of Max Sloan. His body from the waist down was gone, torn to bits by the explosion. One of the cell bars had impaled him through the stomach, another had pierced his chest. Only a shred of flesh held his head to his shoulders. His eyes were gone, the empty sockets staring into nothing.

Will swallowed hard.

"Well, at least we know he didn't escape. Leave him be for now. Let's help the other fellers find the third man."

"You found one?" Malachi asked, when they joined him and Eli.

"Half of one, anyway," Jonas answered. "Still got one more to go."

"He's gotta be somewhere in this mess," Eli said.

The men dug through the rubble for another thirty minutes, until they uncovered another mattress. This one was leaning at an angle against the back wall. A pair of booted feet stuck out from under it. Eli and Malachi flipped the mattress off the man underneath it. Will hunkered next to him.

"He's still alive. Eli, get the doc. If he can't come this instant, find some water or whiskey."

"Right away."

"You think he's got a chance, Ranger?" Malachi asked.

"Hard to say," Will answered. "He's got a lot of cuts and bruises, but they don't look too awful bad. I can't tell about internal injuries or concussion. We'll have to see what the doc says."

Eli returned, accompanied by a stooped over man who was in his late seventies. He was completely bald, and clean shaven. Green eyes peered from behind thick pince-nez spectacles. He nodded to Will.

"Dr. Isaac Pomeroy. What have you got here, Ranger?"

"The only survivor from the cells," Will

answered. "I don't know how badly he's hurt."

"Let me take a look."

Pomeroy skinned back the prisoner's eyelids.

"His pupils aren't dilated, and they're reacting. That's a good sign."

He took a blue glass bottle from his medical bag and removed the lid.

"Smelling salts. These should bring him around."

Pomeroy held the bottle under the prisoner's nose. It wrinkled, and his eyes fluttered open. Pomeroy made the man take another deep whiff from the bottle.

"Good. Those brought you around, mister. I'm the town doctor. I can't say for certain until I examine you more thoroughly, but offhand I'd say you should recover. I'll be back shortly. I'm still treating a more severely injured man."

"Can he answer questions, Doc?" Will asked.

"I don't see why not. Just don't overtax him."

"*Bueno*. I'm obliged."

"Mister, do you remember what happened?" Will asked the prisoner.

"Yep. I sure can. That son of a bitch Sloan knew you had him dead to rights. Swore he would never go to prison for the rest of his life, or hang. He blew himself up, and wanted to take the rest of us with him, especially you, Ranger."

"How?"

"He had a stick of dynamite hidden in the lining

95

of his boot. I didn't realize that until he lit the fuse. Didn't have time to shout a warning. All I could do was pull the mattress over me and hope to Hell it'd save my hide."

"You would have been better off prayin' to God," Jonas said.

"With all the wrong things I've done, I figured He'd never listen to me."

"It's never too late to change your ways, and ask His forgiveness. If anyone should know that, I should. His keeping you alive today is your second chance."

"Jonas, I'm goin' out front to check on things there," Will said. "You stay here with this *hombre* until I get back. Eli and Malachi, if you don't have a problem with digging some more, to see if you turn up any more body parts, I'd appreciate it."

"We'll do it, Ranger," Eli answered.

"*Gracias.*"

Bob Tucker had been dug out of the rubble. The deputy was unconscious, lying face down on a table that had been righted. His shirt had been cut away. A thick splinter, about ten inches long, protruded from his upper left back. Doctor Pomeroy was placing his instruments in a pan of alcohol. He glanced up at Will.

"That man still alive?"

Will nodded.

"He is. Turns out the leader of the bunch committed suicide, by settin' off a stick of dynamite he'd hidden in his boot. Wanted to take everyone in the building with him. He came damn close to succeeding. How's the deputy?"

Pomeroy shook his head.

"It's gonna be touch and go. If I can find all the splinters inside him, that'll mean less chance of infection, and a better chance of survival. If I can't . . ."

Pomeroy's voice trailed off. He shrugged.

"Ranger, I'm about to start working on him. Would you help hold him down? He's probably gonna come to when I begin. It'll take a lot to keep him still. I can't have him jerking around at the wrong moment."

"Sure. Be glad to."

Will took his place between two other men, at Tucker's right side.

"Get ready. Here goes," Pomeroy said.

He doused the wound in Tucker's back with alcohol. The burning pain jolted the deputy awake. He screamed, and tried to writhe away.

"Hold him steady," Pomeroy ordered. "Bob, listen to me. You've got a piece of wood stuck in your back. But, you got lucky. I don't think it hit anything vital. I've got to get it out, though. It's gonna hurt like hell while I work on you. I can't give you laudanum until I'm finished. You might throw up, and choke on your own vomit if

97

I do. You need to hold still as you can. If you jerk away at the wrong moment, that could kill you. Understand?"

Tucker nodded.

"Good."

Pomeroy pulled the splinter out of Tucker's back. When he did, blood flowed freely from the wound. He stuffed a towel into it, until the flow was stanched considerably.

"Now I can see most of what's left inside you, Bob." Under his breath, Pomeroy added, "I hope."

Pomeroy worked on the deputy for over thirty minutes, removing more than a dozen splinters, ranging in length from less than an eighth-of-an-inch to three inches or more.

"I think I've got them all, Bob," he said. "I'll pack the wound, then sew it up."

He wiped out the wound with an alcohol-soaked cloth. He sprinkled some cigarette tobacco into it, then stitched the edges together. He doused the wound with more alcohol.

"I've done everything I can, Deputy. The only worry now is infection. You'll need to stay at my office for a few days, at least. As soon as I get you down there, I'll give you some laudanum, to ease the pain and help you sleep."

"Thanks, Doc."

"If you don't need me any longer, I'd like to get back with my pardner," Will said. "I might have some questions for you later."

"No, go ahead," Pomeroy said. "I've already sent for Marvin Holt, the hardware store owner. He also serves as Cisco's undertaker. It won't take long for me to write up my coroner's report on the dead men."

"No, I reckon not," Will agreed.

The injured had been taken to Doctor Pomeroy's office, the dead to the hardware store/undertaker. The bodies were placed in the storeroom, while Marvin Bolt built coffins for them. They would be buried in unmarked graves at sunrise.

After having their own injuries cared for, Will and Jonas had supper at Cisco and Pancho's Café. Now, they were sitting at a table in the Diablo Saloon, along with Marshal Hanratty and Doc Pomeroy. They were enjoying whiskey while playing a low stakes poker game. Julie Fairchild, the saloon's owner, sat alongside the marshal. Since his arm was indeed broken, now splinted and supported by a sling, she held his cards for him. Fairchild was a stunning redhead, with deep blue eyes. She wore a floor-length, spangled crimson dress that complemented her eyes perfectly. The dress was cut daringly low. It showed off her full cleavage and nicely rounded breasts perfectly. A large red cut-glass gem, dangling from a silver chain, nestled in that cleavage.

Hanratty threw four aces and a king on the table.

"Looks like I win again," he said, as he raked in the pot.

"Marshal, you haven't lost a single hand since your lady friend joined us," Jonas complained.

"She's my good luck charm, all right."

Julie kissed Hanratty on his cheek.

"That's why I keep telling you that we should get married, Jep."

"Uh-uh." Hanratty shook his head. "I like things just the way they are between us. Besides, gettin' married might change my good fortune . . . to plumb bad."

"I keep telling you I'm available, Julie," Pomeroy said.

"And if my mother were still alive she'd be perfect for you, Isaac," Julie retorted. She picked up the whiskey bottle from the center of the table.

"This one's empty. I'll go get another."

Joe Culley, the ill-fated train's engineer, pushed through the batwings. He glanced around the room. Once he spotted Will and Jonas, he hurried over.

"Howdy, Joe," Will said. "You don't seem any the worse for wear."

"No, I'm not. Me 'n Charlie are both just fine, thanks to you and your partner."

"You want to have a drink, and sit in on a couple of hands, Joe?" Hanratty asked.

"I'd like to, but no thanks, Marshal. I don't have the time. I just came over to tell the Rangers some bad news. Ol' Number 10 needs a bit more fixin' than we figured. One of the bullets punctured a steam tube. We won't be ready to roll again until late tomorrow afternoon, at the earliest."

Will and Jonas looked at each other.

"That won't matter," Will said. "We've decided to go the rest of the way to Sweetwater on horseback."

"Are you certain?"

"Yep. We have to wait here until the U.S. Deputy Marshal arrives to take custody of the gold shipment anyway. Since the next train's not due until the day after tomorrow, you'll have to go on without us."

"Besides, the way things have been goin', we'll probably still get to Sweetwater before your train does, Joe," Jonas said.

Culley gave a rueful smile.

"I hate to admit it, but you're most likely right," he said. "I've got to get back to the depot. You boys be careful. Mebbe I'll see y'all in Sweetwater."

"Same goes for you and Charlie," Will said. "Good luck. *Adios*."

"*Adios*."

Julie returned with a new bottle. She filled everyone's glasses.

"I hope you boys are still thirsty."

"We sure are," Pomeroy said.

"Whose deal?" Hanratty asked.

"I believe it's mine."

Jonas picked up the cards and shuffled.

7

Two days later, Will and Jonas rode out of Cisco. Pete and Rebel, after two days of stall rest and plenty of oats, were eager to run, so after they warmed up, their riders let them gallop for half-a-mile, then pulled them down to a steady, mile-eating lope. The Rangers stopped just before high noon for a meal of biscuits and jerky, washed down with warm water from their canteens.

"We can make Abilene tonight," Will said. "Would you rather spend the night in town, or just go on around, and make a camp for the night?"

"Pard, the way things have gone so far, the fewer people and towns I see, the better; leastwise, until we get where we're goin'," Jonas answered. "Especially a rowdy cow town and railhead like Abilene. If it's all the same to you, sleepin' out under the stars suits me just fine. We should be able to scare up a jackrabbit, or a couple of sage hens for supper."

"My thinking exactly," Will answered. "If we get far enough along, we'll swing wide and go past town before we stop. Otherwise, we'll camp a few miles before Abilene, then light out at sunup."

They finished their brief meal, got back in their

saddles, and started riding again. They'd gone about three miles when Will reined Pete in.

"Hold up a minute, Jonas."

Jonas pulled Rebel to a halt.

"Somethin' wrong?"

"No, I've just been thinking. This might take an extra day, might not, but I think we should go by way of Buffalo Gap."

"I've got no quarrel with that. Any particular reason?"

"Yeah. When the railroad bypassed Buffalo Gap, most of the population picked up and moved to Abilene. There are still some folks left. I've heard tell outlaws passin' through town can count on help from some of those folks. Might could be we'll run across a shady character or two."

"In Texas? I don't see how that's possible, pard."

"Yeah." Will gave him a wry grin. "Look, we won't make Buffalo Gap tonight, leastwise not without ridin' these horse most near to death. We'll travel another twenty miles or thereabouts, then make camp. We can spend tomorrow night in town, then move on to Sweetwater after that."

"Sounds like as good a plan as any," Jonas said. "Let's go."

He kicked Rebel into a lope.

"Will, we haven't seen another soul since you decided to head for Buffalo Gap," Jonas said,

.nree hours later. "Are you certain we didn't miss a turn somewhere?"

"No, this is the right trail," Will assured him. "Once the T & P chose to route their tracks north of Buffalo Gap, and established a town site at Abilene, most travelers started usin' the more direct road to Abilene, which runs almost due north. We're cuttin' cross country on the old road from Ranger."

"Sure is lonesome country."

Will laughed.

"I know. The only *hombres* we're liable to run across out here are horse thieves and cattle rustlers. That's another reason I decided to come this way."

"We haven't had any trouble findin' those already, and we haven't even gotten where we're headed for," Jonas said. "Seems to me we don't need to be lookin' for any more renegades. They're been doin' a damn fine job of findin' us, all on their own."

Will laughed again.

"That's what we're paid for, pardner. Unless, of ourse, you'd rather quit, break your probation, d take your chances in Huntsville."

onas shook his head.

"h-uh. Not a chance. At least here I can get from the bad guys. Behind bars, there'd be ape."

's right smart thinkin'."

"How much longer you figure on goin' today?"

Will pushed back his hat and looked up at the sky.

"It's about two hours to sundown. There's a couple of creeks about ten miles ahead. We'll call it a night at one of those."

"That sounds fine to me."

"How much farther?" Jonas asked, slightly over an hour later.

"I've been settin' a slower pace in this heat," Will answered. "Probably three more miles or thereabouts. Hold on."

He pulled Pete to a quick halt. The paint snorted in protest.

"You hear anythin', Jonas?"

"Yeah. Sounds like a herd of cows. Comin' up fast. Stampede?"

"I doubt it. No reason for cows to stampede in this heat. More likely they're bein' shoved along."

"Rustlers?"

"That's my guess. Let's duck into the brush until we see what we're up against."

They moved off the trail, into a bosque mesquite and pin oaks. The thunder of approaching herd grew nearer. Now, the neigh and whinnies of horses drifted on the air.

"Those ain't cows," Jonas said. "Th horses."

"Only *hombres* who'd push broncs like that are horse thieves," Will said. "I'd bet my hat they pushed those animals all night, stopped until now, and have just started out again. Reckon it's up to us to stop 'em. We'll wait until they're just about on top of us, then block the trail and surprise 'em."

He and Jonas pulled out their rifles, and laid them across the pommels of their saddles. They waited, listening as the herd approached.

"Will, it sounds like they're slowin' down," Jonas said.

"They are. They also seem to be turnin' off the trail. We'll wait a couple of minutes, then pick up their tracks. It won't be hard to follow 'em."

After a few minutes, the hoof beats faded. The horses could still be heard, milling around and whinnying.

"Sounds like they might've picked a spot to pen those broncs for the night," Jonas said.

"More likely they already had it chosen," Will answered. "They'll be expectin' trouble, so we've got to play this hand close to our vests. We'll ride in there, slow and friendly-like, and see what happens. There's an off chance those might be honest wranglers, movin' a herd. But no matter what, they'll be suspicious, and on the prod. Be ready when the shootin' starts."

"You mean if."

"No, I mean when."

They replaced their rifles in their saddle scabbards, and emerged back onto the trail. Half-a-mile later, they came upon the hoof prints of a large herd of horses, which turned to the right, following a shallow creek into an *arroyo*.

"That draw's probably a box, Jonas," Will whispered. "The creek most likely starts from a spring at its head. We'll go in real easy. Just be ready for anything."

"Like a bullet in the back?"

"Mebbeso."

They turned into the *arroyo*. Keeping their hands well away from their weapons, they approached the herd.

There was no spot where a lookout might be hidden, so the Rangers rode directly up to the men with the herd. Three mounted men watched the horses as they drank and began grazing. They had stretched ropes across the *arroyo* to keep the herd penned for the night.

"Howdy!" Will called out. "Mind if we come on in?"

The three men looked at each other, then at Will and Jonas.

"You two alone?" the apparent leader asked.

Will smiled and nodded.

"Yes, sir. We're headed for Buffalo Gap, but since we can't get there before dark, we figured to camp by this creek. We heard the ruckus those horses were makin', and figured it wouldn't do to have you be surprised by findin' us camped just below."

"A lot of *muy malo hombres* ride through Buffalo Gap, or so I've heard tell."

"I reckon I've heard tell of that, too," Will answered. "But me'n my pard are just saddle tramps, ridin' the chuck line and seein' the country. My handle's Will. My pard's Jonas."

"Clete Hawkins. My *compadres* are Deke Cannon and Pablo Montoya."

"Good to meet you fellers. That's a nice lookin' bunch of horses you got there."

"They sure are. We'd hate to think anyone'd try and steal 'em from us."

"You've got no worries about that from us, Mr. Hawkins," Will said. "Hell, if you're that concerned, we can just drift on outta here."

"And bring your gang back?" Cannon said. "You must think we're stupid or loco . . . or both."

"Like I said, it's just me and Jonas."

"Jonas don't talk much, does he?"

"Only when I've got somethin' to say."

"That's why I like ridin' with him," Will said. "He don't jabber all day long, bendin' my ears. But he does admire good horse flesh. I see yours are wearin' the Double Diamond brand. Heard that's a good outfit to ride for."

"We wouldn't know," Hawkins said. "We bought these horses from that spread. Takin' 'em up to Cisco. We're meetin' a buyer from the Army there."

"That makes sense," Will said. "The cavalry's always lookin' for good horses. Those hot-blooded thoroughbreds the bluebellies ride ain't fit for the conditions out here. You'll turn a tidy profit."

"Mister, you talk too much," Cannon said.

"Sorry, friend. I'm about done. Oh, just one more thing. Texas Rangers. I don't suppose you boys have a bill of sale for those Double Diamond broncs, by any chance. I'll need to see it."

"Damn *Tejano Diablos*!" Montoya cursed.

"Take it easy, Pablo," Hawkins said. "Ranger, of course I've got a bill of sale. It's right here."

Hawkins grabbed for his six-gun. Before he cleared leather, Will shot him in the belly. Hawkins slumped over his horse's neck.

Cannon had his gun out and leveled. Before he could cock the hammer and pull the trigger, Jonas put a bullet into his chest. Cannon fell from his horse to land face-down in the dirt.

Montoya had his gun half out of his holster, but froze when Will and Jonas pointed their pistols at him.

"You might want to drop that gun, real slow," Will said.

Montoya hesitated.

"Now!" Will snapped.

"Aw, hell. You *gringos* will hang me anyway."

Montoya lifted his gun. Will and Jonas fired simultaneously, both their bullets finding Montoya's chest. He toppled sideways, then slid off his horse.

Hawkins tried to push himself upright. His strength failed him. He tumbled to the ground.

"Jonas, calm those horses before they break outta there," Will ordered. "I'll check these *hombres*."

"Right."

Jonas rode over to the nervously milling horses. Will dropped from his horse. He checked Cannon and Montoya. They were already dead. He walked over to Hawkins, and used the toe of his boot to roll the horse thief onto his back. Hawkins glared at him, his eyes filled with hate.

"Damn. Why'd you have to gut-shoot me, Ranger?"

"It was you or me, and it sure wasn't gonna be me," Will said. "You were too fast. Didn't have time to aim any higher."

Hawkins's breaths were shallow, coming more rapidly as he bled profusely. He struggled to get out his final words.

"Should've . . . kept to our . . . plan to go straight to . . . Abilene. Only travel at night. But the Double Diamond was hard on . . . our trail. We finally . . . slipped away . . . this morning . . . Couldn't chance . . . they'd catch up. Never figured on . . . comin' across . . . Rangers."

Hawkins gasped and stiffened, then went slack. Will straightened up, reloaded his Colt, and slid it back in its holster.

The stolen horses had settled down, most of them grazing at the lush grass along the creek. Jonas rode back and dismounted.

"They all finished?" he asked.

"Yeah. They're done for."

"What now?"

"We'll roll up these *hombres* in their blankets. Looks like we'll have to haul their sorry carcasses into Buffalo Gap come morning. After that, we'll see to our horses, then clean up and make supper."

"I'll strip the gear off those horse thieves' broncs, too," Jonas said. "I don't reckon they should be turned in with the others, though. Otherwise, we'd have to rope them out in the mornin'."

"No, you're right. We'll picket them with Rebel and Pete. We've also got to be ready if the men from the Double Diamond show up. If they do, we'd better hope they're not the type to shoot first and ask questions later."

"You figure they're still followin' these renegades?"

"I'm positive they are. Probably comin' on slow and steady. They won't have to worry about

112

losin' the trail, and by not pushin' their horses too hard, they can travel a lot farther without stoppin'. My guess is they'll quit and take a few hours' break tonight, then start out again an hour or two before sunup, soon as there's enough light to see."

"You don't think they'll ride all night, if they have to? I'd hate to be caught settin'."

"I doubt it. It'd be too easy for them to ride into an ambush. Well, it would have been. Just in case, we'll build a good sized campfire, and keep it burnin' all night. No one would figure a bunch of horse thieves would build a fire at all, let alone one that can be seen for miles. And of course, we'll sleep outside the firelight."

"What time do you plan on lightin' out?"

"Just after sunup. Movin' that herd's gonna slow us down considerable. I reckon it won't be too long until we meet up with the Double Diamond crew. I want them to see those bodies. That should hold off any shootin' long enough until we can explain what happened."

"We'll also be headin' toward them, not away," Jonas pointed out.

"You're gettin' smarter and smarter every day," Will said. "That's right. We'll also raise our hands soon as they spot us. It's unlikely they'd gun us down without askin' questions first. Besides, most ranchers would rather hang rustlers and horse thieves than shoot 'em."

"Somehow, that doesn't give me much comfort, Will," Jonas said.

"That's why you'll stay behind the herd. It'd be hard for those wranglers to get a good shot at both of us. Plus, they wouldn't want to chance hittin' any of their horses by mistake."

"So I get to eat dust tomorrow, mebbe all the way to Buffalo Gap."

"Look at it this way, Jonas. I'll be out front. If a shootin' scrape starts, I'll be the one to eat lead."

"When you put it that way, eatin' dust don't seem bad at all."

"I knew you'd see reason. Now, let's get these *hombres* covered so we can have our supper, then some shut-eye."

8

Will and Jonas were about six miles out of Buffalo Gap, when they saw a cloud of dust on the horizon. Will reined Pete to a stop, the horse herd behind him also halting. Most of the horses dropped their noses to the ground, and began nibbling at the sparse grass. Jonas, leading the horses carrying the dead outlaws, rode up to Will.

"You reckon that's the boys from the Double Diamond, still searchin' for their stolen horses, Will?" he asked.

"I damn sure wouldn't bet against it," Will answered. "Whoever it is, they're comin' closer. I'd say they're still about twenty minutes away. Listen, I've got an idea. You stay up front here, with me. Most likely when whoever's leading the outfit sees those three bodies, they'll be curious. Gives us better odds they'll want to ask a few questions before they start shootin'."

"I'm for that. I'd much prefer answerin' their questions than takin' a bullet in my brisket. 'Course, I'm still gonna have my rifle handy."

"You'd better."

Both men took out their Winchesters and laid them across the pommels of their saddles. Pete and Rebel both tugged at their reins, also desiring to nibble at the grass. Their riders kept the horses' heads high, in case they needed to move quickly.

The terrain here was almost level, so the oncoming riders came into view from nearly a mile away. They continued at a quick pace until they drew within rifle range. The leader raised his hand for the men with him to stop. All of them placed their hands on the butts of their revolvers.

"Howdy, men," Will said. "You happen to be lookin' for these here Double Diamond horses? Seems the ones you're ridin' are wearin' the same brand."

"That's for damn certain we're after those broncs. They belong to me. They were stolen right off my range," the leader replied. "They're a good chunk of my outfit's *remuda*. You mind tellin' me what you're doin' with 'em, before we shoot you out of your saddles?"

"Not at all, although that might not be as easy as you think, even though you've got us outnumbered three to one. We're Texas Rangers. I'm Will Kirkpatrick. My pardner's Jonas Peterson. Those three *hombres*, lyin' belly down over the horses Jonas is holding, should give you a good idea."

"You're Rangers? Got any proof?"

"We've got our commissions right in our shirt pockets, if you want to see 'em."

"Nope. I'll take your word for it. Too easy for a man to get plugged while he's reaching for somethin' another man's handing him. If you're not who you claim to be, we'll find out soon enough. Then you'll swing from the nearest tree. I'm Dave Diamond, owner of the Double Diamond. The man next to me is Raoul Castaneda, my foreman."

"Pleased to meet y'all," Will said.

"*I'm* pleased you got our horses back, and took care of the sons of bitches who stole 'em," Diamond said. "How'd it happen?"

"We're on our way farther west, on an assignment," Will answered, not wanting to divulge any more information. "We were about to stop and make camp for the night when we heard a bunch of animals, bein' pushed hard. We slipped into the brush to see what it was all about. Before the horse thieves reached us, they turned into a box *arroyo*. We followed 'em. When we asked where they got the horses, they claimed they bought 'em, and we're gonna sell 'em to the Army. I told the man in charge we were Rangers. Asked him for a bill of sale. Instead, he and his compadres went for their guns. Bad mistake. It was already too late to travel much farther before dusk, so we spent the night, then started out for Buffalo Gap at sunup. Figured you'd be on their trail, and we'd come across you. If not, we would have left the herd in Buffalo Gap, and gotten word to you."

"*Muchas gracias*. We're beholden to you," Diamond said.

"All part of the job," Jonas answered.

"We'll turn your horses over to you now," Will said. "Seein' as there won't be a trial, we don't have to hold them for evidence."

"Appreciate that. Would y'all like to ride back to the ranch with us? My wife is a real good cook. You'd be welcome to spend the night in the bunkhouse."

"We're grateful for the offer, Mr. Diamond, but we're in kind of a hurry to reach our destination," Will answered. "We'll ride into Buffalo Gap, spend the night there, then push on. Maybe some other time."

"I understand," Diamond said. "You'll be welcome anytime. What about those dead *hombres*? You want us to take 'em off your hands? It'd be a real pleasure to plant 'em, or just dump those bastards for the buzzards and coyotes."

"No thanks. We'll take 'em into Buffalo Gap, and let the town bury 'em. We want this to be a warning, that the Rangers are patrolling the territory, and lawbreakers better skedaddle out of Texas, or end up like these three."

"You'll have your hands full, that's for certain, Ranger. Good luck."

"You'll need it," Castaneda added.

"We'll take those horses off your hands now, Rangers," Diamond said. "Bobby, Mitch, take the drag. George, Hank, you take the flanks. Me'n Raoul will ride point. Rangers, thanks again. *Vaya con Dios.*"

"*Adios*," Will answered. Leaving the Double Diamond crew to gather their horses, he and Jonas resumed their journey.

Will and Jonas rode into Buffalo Gap late that afternoon. Many of the town's buildings had been disassembled, then moved to Abilene and rebuilt. Most of the remaining structures were abandoned, the residents and business owners having followed the Texas and Pacific to Abilene.

There was a general store, a few small shops, and a building marked Town Offices, Marshal's Office, and Jail. There was a two-story structure which was occupied by the Buffalo Gap Hotel, as well as the town's sole remaining saloon and café. Alongside that was the livery stable.

The few people on the street dropped what they were doing to watch the Rangers, as they rode up to the marshal's office, dismounted, and tied their horses. The marshal, an elderly man with long gray hair, beard, and moustache, stepped outside. He was cadaverously thin. When he started to speak, he broke into a spasm of painful coughing, then spit blood and thick green phlegm into the street. He was clearly in the latter stages of consumption.

"What's this all about?" he asked. "I don't appreciate strangers ridin' into my town, totin' three dead men along behind 'em."

"Texas Rangers Will Kirkpatrick and Jonas

Peterson," Will said. "We found these three *hombres* with a good-sized number of stolen horses from the Double Diamond spread. We tried to arrest 'em, peaceable like. They weren't havin' none of that."

"And just might where those horses be now?"

"Dave Diamond and a few of his men were trailin' these *hombres*. We returned his horses to them. We'd appreciate it if you'd take the bodies off our hands for buryin'. And let us use your office to write up our report and get it mailed off, unless there's a telegraph office in town."

"Western Union pulled up stakes when the railroad bypassed us, Ranger," one of the bystanders said. "I'm Roger Watson, owner of the Buffalo Gap Hotel. I'm also the town postmaster, and the de facto mayor. The Post Office is in the hotel lobby. Writin' up your report there is far preferable to usin' Marshal Frost's office. Abe doesn't exactly keep it clean."

"It's clean enough for me, since Tillie passed," Frost said. "A man needs a wife to keep a place tidied up."

"We appreciate the offer, Mr. Watson," Will said. "Thanks. Marshal, where do you want these bodies?"

"The Rangers gonna take care of the bill? This town can't afford to bury 'em."

"Nope, I'm afraid plantin' these men is the town's responsibility," Will answered. "You can try'n bill the county, if you want. Won't take more'n a couple of men with shovels, anyway. Nobody's gonna care if three horse thieves have markers for their graves. The town can also claim their horses and gear as compensation. That should more than cover the buryin' expenses, with some left over for the town coffers."

"Abe, that's fine," Watson said. "Any of you men want to make three dollars? Dollar a grave, plus free beers at the saloon once the chore is finished."

Four men raised their hands.

"Good. Mel, I don't see Purdy here. Tell him I said to loan you four shovels. I'll pay him a quarter rental fee for each. Ben, Chuck, Ed, take the bodies off the Rangers' hands. Ranger . . ."

"Kirkpatrick," Will repeated. "And Peterson."

"Thank you. Soon as you get your horses stalls, there's rooms at the hotel available for you, if you're planning on spending the night. We don't see many travelers in Buffalo Gap nowadays."

"As a matter of fact, we are," Will said. "A bed, meal, and a roof over our heads, will be a nice change from bacon and beans for supper, and the hard ground for a mattress."

"Excellent. I'll see you in the lobby."

Once the horses carrying the dead horse thieves were led away, Will and Jonas rode to the livery stable. A man about the marshal's age, but with a much healthier appearance, and a muscular build, was waiting for them.

"Howdy, men," he said. "I saw you ride in, and seen what happened at the marshal's office. Name's Hezekiah Jones, but everyone calls me Jonesy. You'll be wantin' stalls for your animals for the night."

"And a good rubdown and feedin'," Will said. He swung out of his saddle, as did Jonas. "I'm Will, and this here's Pete. Treat him good."

"I'm Jonas, my horse is Rebel. He's a mite touchy about his legs, so be careful when you brush them down," Jonas warned.

"They'll both be fine," Jonesy assured both men. "Horses in my care get nothin' but the best. They'll have a good helpin' of oats, and plenty of hay. Four bits each. Just grab your gear and I'll take those cayuses from here. Cleanin' your saddles and bridles is also included. No extra charge."

"Much obliged, Jonesy," Will said. He and Jonas removed their saddlebags, slung them over their shoulders, and took their rifles. Will gave Pete a licorice, while Jonas gave Rebel a piece of leftover biscuit. Satisfied their horses were in good hands, they walked to the hotel. Roger Watson was at the front desk, waiting for them as promised. With him was a blonde, hazel-eyed woman about his age, who still had a pretty face and well-formed figure. She wore a high collared, conservative dress of dove gray velvet. She smiled at the Rangers' approach.

"Gentlemen, welcome to the Buffalo Gap Hotel," she said. "Roger told me to expect you."

"This is Susannah, my wife," Watson said. "Susannah, Rangers Kirkpatrick and Peterson."

"Ma'am." Will touched the brim of his hat in greeting, as did Jonas.

"You'll want two rooms," she said. "If you'll just sign the register. Usually, the price is one dollar a night, but since the hotel is mostly empty, and you're peace officers, you may have them for fifty cents each."

"That's right generous of you, Mrs. Watson," Jonas said. He and Will signed for their rooms, paid, then Mrs. Watson handed them their keys.

"Ranger Kirkpatrick, you'll be in Room 6. Ranger Peterson, yours is the one next to his, Room 8. I'll have some hot water and towels sent up, so you can wash before supper. We start serving at five-thirty."

"With your permission, Susannah and I would like the privilege of dining with you," Watson said. "Say at six?"

"That'll be just fine," Will answered.

"Excellent. We'll see you then."

Will and Jonas went up to their rooms. Will unlocked the door to his and looked inside.

"Say, this looks pretty nice, pard," he said to Jonas. "Even has a rug on the floor."

"I'm just happy we don't have to share a bed for once," Jonas answered. "I won't have to listen to you snorin' all night long. You could wake a dead man."

"And I won't have to put up with your jabbin' your elbow in my ribs," Will retorted. "We've got a couple of hours until supper. After I clean up, I'm gonna take a nap."

"What about writin' up the report?"

"Oh, yeah. That won't take long. I'll see you at six."

"See you then."

Roger and Susannah Watson proved to be charming hosts. They insisted all conversation be kept light until the meal was complete. Now, after a sumptuous repast of roast beef, mashed potatoes and gravy, accompanied by black-eyed peas, with pecan pie for dessert, they were all enjoying second cups of coffee. Will, Jonas, and Watson were also smoking cigars, provided by the hotel owner.

"Will, you don't have to answer if you can't, or would prefer not to, but where are you headed when you leave here?" Watson asked.

"Sweetwater, for starters. After that, it all depends on where the outlaws we're after lead us."

"We're not after any particular man, or gang," Jonas added. "Our orders are to clear out as many renegades as we can, by any means necessary."

"That's one reason we brought those horse thieves' bodies here for burying, rather than having the Double Diamond crew handling that chore, or leavin' 'em for the scavengers," Will added. "It was to serve as a warning. With luck, it will give second thoughts to others who might get similar ideas. It sounds harsh, but it's effective."

"You have a tough job ahead of you, then," Mrs. Watson said. "Lord knows we have enough criminals come through Buffalo Gap. Of course, it doesn't help our situation when the marshal is an elderly man, who can no longer handle the job. Yet the town council refuses to replace him. If I were mayor, you can be certain there would be a change. And if women were allowed to vote, I'd run for mayor. I'd be elected, too. Then you'd see some changes in this town."

"Now, Susannah, we've had this discussion before," Watson said. "The town can't afford to pay more money for a new marshal. Also, do I need to remind you again that politics is not something for the fairer sex to be involved with? It's unseemly, unladylike, and not at all feminine. Gentlemen, I'm afraid I must apologize for my wife's outspokenness."

"There's no apology necessary," Will said. "Outlawry is often harder on the womenfolks than the men. It's women who will civilize the frontier."

"My pardner has a good point," Jonas said. "Us men certainly don't seem to be doing a good job of running things."

"See, Roger? Even our guests agree with me."

Will decided to change the subject, before things became even more uncomfortable.

"Mr. Watson, you certainly aren't from around these parts," he said. "How did you end up in Buffalo Gap, Texas, of all places?"

"No, I'm not," Watson answered. "I'm originally from New Jersey, my wife is from New York City. We both decided we wanted to leave that life behind. When we first came to Buffalo Gap, the hotel was for sale. We bought it on the spot, because we fell in love with this little town. When the railroad bypassed us, we decided not to follow the majority of the residents, who packed up, lock, stock, and barrel, and moved to Abilene. We've never regretted our choice."

"No, we haven't," Mrs. Watson agreed. "What's that saying? Better to be a big fish in a little pond, or a little fish in a big pond?"

"Or frog," Jonas added.

"Anyway, we're both happy here," Mrs. Watson continued. "The hotel, dining room, and saloon provide us a decent living. Yes, there is some trouble with ruffians now and again, more so since the railroad went north of us, but they usually move on after one or two nights. There's no real reason for them to remain here. You can see there's not much for entertainment in Buffalo Gap."

"Sometimes it's better not enough than too much," Will said. "But speaking of entertainment, me'n Jonas thank you for supper. We're obliged. Tell your cook it was real tasty. We figure we'll have a couple of drinks at the saloon before we turn in."

"You're quite welcome," Watson answered. "Enjoy yourselves. I hope you won't think us rude, but Susannah and I retire to our suite immediately after supper. She does her needle-point, while I work on the ledgers, or read a book."

"Of course, we understand," Will answered. "We're gonna turn in early ourselves, since we'll be ridin' out not much after first light."

"Then we'll say good night," Mrs. Watson said. "Have a pleasant night's sleep."

"Thank you. *Buenas noches.*"

Having said their good nights, Will and Jonas made their way to the next-door saloon.

The Buffalo Gap Saloon was smaller than most establishments of its type. It had the usual mirror-backed bar, but only a few tables. There was no house gambler, nor any set-ups for faro, roulette wheels, or chuck-a-luck cages. There were just two card tables, and no piano or dance floor. There were also no women, just a bartender and his assistant.

By nine o'clock, there were only a few patrons at the bar, including Will and Jonas. Jonesy, the livery stable owner, was at one of the card tables with three cowboys from local ranches. They were drinking beer and playing a low-stakes game of five card stud.

Will drained the last of his whiskey, and set the glass on the bar.

"One more, Charlie, then me'n Jonas are gonna call it a night," he said to the bartender.

"Sure thing, Ranger."

Charlie refilled their glasses. As Will took his first sip, three men rode up, stopped their horses in front of the saloon, dismounted, and tied them to the rail. Will glanced in the back bar mirror when they pushed their way through the swinging doors. He nudged his elbow into Jonas's ribs. He waited until the men were halfway to the bar, then turned to face them. He stood casually, his elbows resting on the bar. Alongside him, Jonas stood, alert and watchful.

"Well, if it ain't Ben K. Green," Will said. "And your old pardners are still with you. It's been a while."

"Will Kirkpatrick. Of all the damn luck," Green said. "Out of all the towns in Texas, I come across you here. Who's the kid with you?"

"Him? He's my new ridin' *compadre*, Jonas Peterson. Jonas, meet Ben Green, and his pardners, Glen Bartlett and Bedford Hart."

Bartlett snorted, then laughed.

"That young'n's a Texas Ranger! Hell, he ain't even old enough to shave. That gun on his hip's too big for a skinny boy like him. I'm surprised it doesn't pull you right over, kid. I'll bet you can't even lift it, sonny."

"Jonas, Bartlett always did have a big mouth," Will said. "Now's the time I should probably explain the law's been lookin' for these sons of bitches for a long time. Murder and bank robbery, among other charges. Not to mention breakin' jail, while they were awaitin' trial for cattle rustlin'. I'm the one who put them behind bars for that. Green, you and your men are under arrest."

Green laughed.

"There's three of us and one of you, Kirkpatrick."

"Two of us," Will said, softly. He took his elbows off the bar, and stood straight, his hand hovering over the butt of his Peacemaker. The drinkers on either side scrambled for cover, not wanting to catch a stray bullet. Charlie and his assistant ducked under the bar.

"I'm not countin' that *boy* with you," Green answered, with a sneer. "I figure he'll cut and run as soon as the shootin' starts. Won't do him no good, though. One of us'll put a bullet in his back, soon as we're done with you."

Hart spoke up for the first time.

"He's too damn scared to even move. Probably about to pee his pants. Hasn't said a word. What's the matter, sonny? Cat got your tongue?"

"Ben, before you make your play, lemme take on the kid," Bartlett said. "Just me'n him. I'll teach him how to handle a gun. 'Course, he won't remember his lesson, once I put a bullet right between his eyes."

"That ain't gonna happen," Jonas said, his voice barely above a whisper.

"Hey. The kid *can* talk," Hart said.

"So he can," Green said. "Glen, he's all yours. Go ahead and kill him. Then me'n Bedford'll finish off Kirkpatrick."

"I'm obliged, *amigo*. Boy, you got anythin' to say before I gun you down? Or would you rather try'n make a run for it. Mebbe I won't shoot you if you make it to the door."

"Mr. Bartlett," Jonas began.

"Hey, did y'all hear that, Ben, Bedford? The boy called me *Mister* Bartlett. Ain't that real polite? He knows how to talk to his betters. He's showin' me respect. Almost makes me wish I didn't have to kill him. Go ahead, boy. You wanted to say somethin'?"

"Yep. You see that fourth button down on your shirt? The one just above your gunbelt's buckle? I'm gonna put my first slug right in that button, and send it through your guts and into your backbone. Now, if you don't rile me too much, I'll finish you off quick, with a slug just above where your shirt's unbuttoned. That one should take you plumb in the heart. But if you say one more unkind word about me, I'll just let you die gut-shot, real slow and painful. Don't matter which to me. Either way, you're about to die."

"Why, you snivelin', smart-mouthed son of a bitch!"

Bartlett went for his gun. Jonas easily beat his draw. He lifted his Peacemaker from its holster, thumbed back the hammer, and pulled the trigger. The fourth button on Bartlett's shirt disappeared in a spray of blood. Bartlett dropped his pistol, clamped his hand to his middle, and slumped into a chair. Jonas shifted his gun, and put two bullets through Hart's stomach. Hart dropped on the spot, without taking a step. Before Green could even react, Jonas shifted his gun again, and put two slugs into his belly. Green jackknifed, staggered into the bar, and collapsed to the sawdust covered floor. He rolled onto his back, as blood spread over his shirtfront.

Will had yanked his own gun, but never got the chance to pull the trigger, before all three outlaws were down. Powder smoke filled the air, along with the stench of sulfur.

"He . . . he done kilt me, Ben," Bartlett said, in disbelief.

"He done got . . . all of us," Green gasped. "Damn, I hurt. Kirkpatrick, you got to get us . . . a doctor."

Charlie got up from behind the bar. He leaned over it and peered at Hart.

"There's no doc in this town," he said. "I'm the closest thing to one. I've removed plenty of bullets in my time. But it don't take any doctor to see you three are done for. Not when all three of you are belly shot."

"Ya . . . ya gotta help me," Bartlett pleaded.

"I've still got one bullet left," Jonas said. "But I'm not gonna waste it on the likes of you."

He punched the empties out of his Colt's cylinder and reloaded.

"Thanks for the help, pard," he said to Will, who was checking Hart.

"Didn't seem like you needed any," Will answered. "Besides, the way they were ridin' you, I figured you'd want to have all the fun. I would've stepped in if I had to. This one's already gone."

The back of Hart's shirt was soaked with blood, from two large exit wounds. Will walked over to Green.

"Kirkpatrick . . . I thought mebbe someday . . . you'd kill me, or I'd . . . kill you. Never figured on a . . . snot-nosed kid . . . gettin' me."

Green grabbed his middle, groaned in pain, and rolled onto his side. His breathing ceased.

Bartlett's arms dropped to his side. His breaths rattled in his chest, and blood flowed from his mouth. With one final effort, he tried to stand, but rolled off the chair, dead.

Will and Jonas slid their pistols back into their holsters, as the other patrons came out from cover, behind overturned tables and chairs.

"Kid, that was some kinda shootin'," Jonesy said. "Ain't seen nothin' like it in my entire life, and I'm an old man."

"I didn't have much choice," Jonas answered. "Besides, Will's faster."

"Don't see how."

"Trust me, he is. He could take me, easy."

"Yeah, I probably could, but gut-shootin' three men, Jonas?" Will said. "That was just plain mean."

"Well, they shouldn't've riled me."

"I reckon not," Charlie said. "They won't do it again. That's for damn certain."

Roger Watson hurried down the stairs. He had thrown on pants and a shirt, which was still unbuttoned. He was in stocking feet. He stopped at the bottom of the staircase to observe the scene.

"What the devil happened?" he asked.

"The three men you see lyin' there were wanted for murder and bank robbery. They resisted arrest," Will told him. "Jonas saved the state the cost of a trial, and three hangings. And we've got three more men we can remove from the Rangers' Fugitive List."

"He shot all three of them?"

"He did," Will confirmed. "Didn't seem right for me to get in his way."

"Did anyone send for Mike Purdy, and Marshal Frost?" Watson asked.

"Matt Thornton just left," Charlie answered. "He'll be back with 'em shortly."

"Good. The sooner this mess is cleaned up, the better. I assume this means you won't be leaving as early tomorrow as you planned, Ranger?"

"Perhaps just an hour or so later," Will answered. "We'll need to write up our report and mail it before we leave."

"I'd appreciate that. You seem to have brought nothing but trouble along with you. We're not used to shootings in Buffalo Gap."

"That wouldn't be because outlaws know they're safe here, with the only law being an old man, who's dying of consumption—would it, Mr. Watson? A man who owns a town's sole hotel, saloon, and restaurant could turn a tidy profit by making the place a haven for lawbreakers."

"What are you implying, Ranger?"

"Not a thing," Will said. "Just keep this in mind. Me'n Jonas have been assigned to clean up this area. And we will. Bet your hat on it."

"Is that a threat?"

"No. It's a promise. You'll have to decide which side of the law you want to remain on. But you can count on seeing us again. Jonas, c'mon. There's no need for us to be here, waitin' for these bodies to be hauled off. We'll put that report together, then turn in. I'm certain Mr. Watson will be delighted to open the Post Office early for us."

"You're damn right I will," Watson snapped. Hatred burned in his eyes.

"We're obliged."

Most of the men in the saloon resumed their drinking, and the card game. A couple drifted home once the Rangers headed to their rooms.

"Boy howdy, Watson sure changed his tune when he saw those three dead *hombres*," Jonas said, after they were in Will's room, and the door was closed.

"I suspected he would," Will answered. "He was puttin' on a good show for us, but we spoiled his act when we took care of Green and his pardners. Well, I guess that should be you took care of Green and his pardners."

"I couldn't have done it without knowin' you had my back, Will. But how'd you figure out Watson?"

"Fairly simple. He pretty much runs this town, as you saw. He has to be aware outlaws have been stoppin' here. That's why he doesn't want a new marshal. At least, not until he finds one that will look the other way. Watson's got a good thing here. It's clear Green and his pals thought they'd be safe. They just didn't realize we were in town, or they would have gone right on past. Or more likely, waited and bushwhacked us. You can be certain Watson charges any renegades who come through double what the goin' rate is, for anything they need. He doesn't want to give that up."

"What about his wife?"

"I'm not certain. Even if she is aware of what's goin' on, there's not much she can do about it."

"I guess not," Jonas said. "Let's get this report done, so we can grab some shut-eye."

"Sure. Just got one question for you."

"What's that, Will?"

"You told Jonesy I could take you in a gunfight. Are you certain about that? Because I for damn sure ain't."

"Well, we'd better hope we never have to find out, hadn't we?" Jonas said. He clapped Will on the shoulder and laughed.

9

It was about three in the afternoon, two days later, when Will and Jonas reached Sweetwater. Their first stop was the Nolan County Sheriff's Office. The deputy at the front desk looked up when they walked in.

"Can I help you fellers?" he asked.

"You sure can. Texas Rangers Will Kirkpatrick and Jonas Peterson. Is Sheriff Butler in?"

Will handed their commissions to the deputy, who looked them over, then handed them back.

"He sure is. Wait here, and I'll get him."

The deputy went down a wainscoted corridor and into an office on the left. He returned a few moments later, with a middle-aged, burly man, who was wearing a sheriff's badge on his cowhide vest.

"Howdy, men," the sheriff said. "Moe Butler."

He extended his hand. Will took it. He winced at the power in the sheriff's grip as they shook.

"Will Kirkpatrick."

Butler then extended his hand to Jonas, who also took it.

"Jonas Peterson."

"Glad to see you boys. I'd expected you a few days ago, based on Captain Hunter's message. How's he doin'? We rode together durin' the War."

"He's just fine and sends along his howdy," Will answered. "And we are later gettin' here than planned. There was some trouble on the train. It was delayed so much we decided to get off in Cisco, and take our horses the rest of the way."

"Yeah, the robberies. I heard about those."

"You mean the train actually got here?" Jonas asked.

"Two days ago."

"Damn. You were right, Will. That means I'm buyin' supper tonight."

"Which means I eat real good tonight," Will said, with a laugh. To Butler, he continued, "Another reason we're late is we went around by way of Buffalo Gap. Tangled with some horse thieves, then Ben K. Green and his men."

"You're here, so I assume those men won't be a problem for quite some time."

"More like permanently," Jonas said.

Butler threw back his head and laughed.

"Good old-fashioned Texas Ranger justice. The best kind. Quick and efficient. No loose ends left behind. No decent person'll mourn Green's bunch, that's for certain. Good riddance."

"They didn't give us any choice," Will said.

"Would that have made a difference?"

Will shrugged.

"*Quien sabe*? Mebbe, mebbe not. The powers that be in Buffalo Gap don't seem real interested in what kind of *hombres* come through town. Long as they're willin' to pay, the business owners are willin' to look the other way. Puttin' those renegades behind bars in Buffalo Gap probably would have meant they'd "escape" from jail, a day or two after we left town."

"Well, I'm sure happy to see you Rangers. There's plenty of trouble in this territory for you to handle. Come on back to my office and we'll palaver a spell."

Will and Jonas followed Butler to his office.

"Coffee's on the stove. Cups on the shelf next to it."

The men each filled a tin mug with black coffee. Butler sat behind his desk. Will and Jonas took chairs in front of it. All three rolled and lit cigarettes.

Butler leaned back in his chair.

"I'm aware you've been sent here to clean out the owlhoots plaguin' this whole region," he said. "Where do you plan to start?"

"That's what I'm gonna ask you, Sheriff," Will answered.

"Call me Moe. Y'all don't mind if I call you boys by your first names, I hope."

"Not at all."

"Fine. There's two main problem areas. One is between here and San Angelo. The road from here to there is lousy with highwaymen and stage robbers. My deputies are stretched way too thin to even make a dent in the amount of robberies and killin's there's been on that road. In fact, I've lost three deputies in the past month to drygulchin's on that route. Same with Sheriff Tuttle down in Tom Green County. He doesn't have enough men, and he's had five deputies ambushed. There's talk of cuttin' a new county out of Tom Green, which would sure help, but so far that's all it is, talk. Things are so bad the Army won't even let their men take the stage from here to Fort Concho. Anyone who rides that road alone is just plain suicidal. And of course, there's the usual cattle rustling and horse stealin'."

"All right, so we've got our work cut out for us," Will said. "Where's the other trouble spot?"

"North of here. That's mostly cattle and horse rustlin'. It's pretty easy for just a few *hombres* to rustle a herd of beef, then run it north. They can disappear into the Caprock Canyons. Once they get in those, it's nigh impossible to track 'em. Most men who've tried never come back out again. It's mighty rugged country."

"Any of those rustlers attempted to get into Palo Duro Canyon?" Will asked.

"I dunno," Butler answered. "I suppose some might have tried. They'd have to have a lot of guts, or be really stupid, to try it, though. If any of the hands from Charlie Goodnight's JA Ranch came across 'em on JA range, they'd be hung without question. Plus, it's a lot longer trip to the Indian Territories, not to mention Palo Duro itself. Much quicker to push a stolen herd into the Caprock, hide out there until the pursuers give up, then push 'em east into the Territories. Not too many folks live up that way, and there's no law at all. The settlers know if they want to keep themselves and their families alive, to just look the other way."

"All right, Moe. We'll start to work tomorrow," Will said. "Do you have any preference where?"

"Will, I'd rather have you start south first. That's where most of the killin's have taken place. It's more important to round up cold-blooded murderers than rustlers."

"Including those who bushwhacked eight lawmen," Jonas said.

"That's right. Those are the bastards I want tracked down the most. It eats at my guts every day, knowin' those damn sneakin' back shooters are still on the prowl. They're nothin' but cowards, who don't even have the guts to go up against a man face to face. I don't need to tell you I don't particularly care if you bring 'em back for trial, or not."

"My guess is not," Will said.

"I didn't say that."

"You didn't have to."

"Most of 'em probably won't give up without a fight anyway, knowin' a hemp noose is waitin' for 'em," Jonas said.

"As long as you boys come back, without bein' ventilated," Butler said. "I suppose you'll want a place to spend the night."

"That, stalls for our horses, their shoes replaced, and a good supper," Will answered. "We'd also like to get shaves, haircuts, and baths. We've got to pick up more supplies, too."

"The best hotel is the Moriarty, right across the street," Butler said. "Two doors down from that is the Sweetwater Mercantile. Right next to the store is Ted's Tonsorial Parlor. Pete Christiansen is the town blacksmith and farrier. He also owns the livery stable. His shop and barn are at the end of the street, across the T & P tracks. That should take care of all your needs. Anything else?"

"Yup. Just one more thing. When does the next stage for San Angelo leave?"

"Today's Monday. The stage south left this morning. The next one leaves Thursday. It starts out from up in Wichita Falls. If it's on time, it'll roll in about nine o'clock, and pull out at ten. Wells Fargo changes out the driver and guard here."

"We'll be on it," Will said. "Would it be too much of a favor to ask you to get us a pair of tickets, Moe? I'd like to leave tomorrow before the office opens."

"No, I can do that. You gonna use aliases?"

"No, give the agent our real names. Just don't tell him we're Rangers. I don't want anyone

142

to know who we are, not even the driver and shotgun. Can't chance word getting out, and spookin' off anyone thinkin' of robbin' the stage. Stagecoach drivers love their gossip. If one of 'em gets to drinkin' at the saloon, he might let somethin' slip."

"There's also a chance the driver or guard could be in on the robberies," Jonas said. "Knowin' there's a couple of Rangers on the run would have them call off the job."

"Or gun us down as soon as it started," Will added. "That's why we need complete secrecy."

"Understood," Butler said. "The only ones who'll know who you two are will be myself and Paul Hawkins, my deputy out front. Neither of us'll talk. When I buy the tickets, I'll tell the agent you're old acquaintances of mine, who're headin' south lookin' for work."

"Better yet, say we're lookin' for ranch land to buy, down San Angelo way. If you can drop a hint we're carryin' *dinero* for a deposit, so much the better. That bait should lure a few snakes out of the woodpile."

"I'll let that slip," Butler promised. "If word gets to the right people, it'll be all over town by nightfall."

"Excellent. We're obliged," Will said. "Now, we'd better get movin'. If we spend much more time here, people'll start wonderin' what kind of business we have with the sheriff. Oh, don't even let the town marshal know you met with us."

"You're probably right about that. Lincoln Tuttle's a good man, and he wouldn't talk, but if he doesn't know anything, he damn sure won't have to lie if anyone gets curious about you two, and starts askin' questions."

"Then we're all set. We'll be back in town sometime late Wednesday," Will said. "How much is the fare to San Angelo?"

"Three dollars each. It's gone up considerable since all the trouble started."

Will pulled his billfold from his pocket. He handed the sheriff six one-dollar bank notes.

"That'll cover our tickets. Mebbe, by the time we return, a few outlaws won't be botherin' folks headin' for San Angelo."

"You won't be able to bring them back here. Not without folks figurin' out you're the law," Butler objected.

"Who said anythin' about bringing 'em back?" Will answered. "See you in a couple of days."

10

"You got any particular plan in mind, Will?" Jonas asked, as they rode south out of Sweetwater the next morning. "Or are we just gonna ride around and look at the birdies and the pretty flowers all day long?"

"Ridin' along *is* pretty much the plan," Will answered. "Like we ain't got a care in the world. Just a couple of saddle tramps, with nowhere in particular to go and nothin' particular to do. If we look like we're not payin' attention, some *malo hombres* might decide we're easy pickings. They'll find out they're wrong. Or, it's possible we'll come across someone who's seen something suspicious, or mebbe even been waylaid themselves. So we're just gonna scout around and see what happens."

"What's the country like around here? There doesn't seem to be much cover. It'd be kind of hard to surprise a man."

"It's doggone flat, all right—leastways, right through here. But the land's not as flat as it looks, either. It's got a lot of dips and hollows, that are barely noticeable. When the Comanches ruled this area, they'd lie in wait in shallow dips, hidden by dry grass. A man could ride right up on 'em without even knowing they were there, until it was too late. Some of the renegades we're lookin' for are certain to know that trick. The brush will thicken up, farther down the road. There's also dry washes and some small canyons between here and Sweetwater. Even a couple of low hills or mesas. So there's plenty of spots where a man plannin' an ambush can hide. And that is one thing we can be grateful for, that the Comanch' and Kiowas have been driven out of Texas. There's an occasional stray raidin' party, but most of the Indians are on their reservations, up in the Territories, or they've fled across the Rio Grande into Mexico. We'll be lookin' for white raiders, at least mostly."

"How far you figure on ridin'?"

"Depends. We'll keep on until sundown tonight, camp, then retrace our route tomorrow. We can't afford to miss our stage."

"If we don't come across any outlaws, we'll be wastin' two whole days," Jonas protested.

"That's what most of Rangerin' is," Will answered. "A lot of ridin' around, chasin' men who disappear into the tall and uncut like ghosts. Besides, we won't really be wastin' our time, even if we come up empty-handed. We'll be able to figure out the spots where the stage is most likely to be hit."

"That makes sense. As long as I don't have to get on another train, I'm happy."

"Same here, pard," Will said, laughing. "Same here."

He kicked Pete into a slow jogtrot.

"A couple of riders in the brush up ahead, Jonas," Will said, four miles later.

"I see 'em. Wonder what they're up to."

"I reckon we'll find out. They might've just stopped for a rest, or mebbe to relieve themselves, but I doubt it."

When they drew near the waiting men, they rode out of the brush, to block the Rangers' way.

"Howdy, fellers," one said. "Nice day, ain't it?"

He was in his late twenties, with a sallow complexion, long brown hair, and light brown eyes. His height was about five-foot-nine, his weight about one-seventy-five.

"Yeah, it is," Will answered. "Gonna be a trifle hot, though."

"I've gotta agree with you, cowboy," the second man said. "Hell ain't nothin' compared to Texas heat."

This man was about the same age as his companion, but had a lighter complexion, sun and wind burned. His hair was sandy, his eyes gray. He was about four inches taller and twenty pounds heavier than his partner.

"Where're you boys headin', if you don't mind my askin'?" the sallow-faced man said.

"We do mind, and it's none of your damn business," Jonas snapped.

"Now, Jonas, don't be rude. These men are just bein' friendly, that's all. Ain't that right?"

"That's right," Sallow Face answered.

"My apologies. You'll have to make allowances for my pard," Will said. "He's still a youngster, and hasn't learned to control his tongue yet. We're headed for San Angelo. I've got a brother down there, who's got some land he wants me to look at. We're thinking of startin' a ranch."

"Then it's a good thing you ran across us today," Sandy Hair said. "Dunno if you're aware of it or not, but the road between here and San Angelo is mighty dangerous."

"We've heard stories."

"Probably not as bad as things really are," Sallow Face said. "The robbers and killers are thick as fleas in these parts. We can't possibly let you fellers take this road, without protection."

"We can handle ourselves all right."

"Maybe I didn't make myself clear. We're offerin' you protection. You'd better take our offer. Otherwise, somethin' plumb awful is liable to happen."

"Oh, I see. Just how much will this 'protection' cost? Does it come with a guarantee?"

"Why, sure it does. Nobody'll bother you all the way to San Angelo, if you purchase our services.

It's well worth the hundred dollars apiece we charge."

"Just let me get this clear in my head," Will said. "If we don't pay you men to "protect us', somethin' bad will happen down the road."

"That's right," Sallow Face said, with an unctuous grin. "A feller could get drygulched, real easy. Or his hoss could throw him, or he could get snake bit. All sorts of things."

"Even somethin' like this?"

Will popped his reins across Sallow Face's buckskin gelding's shoulders. The horse reared and spun, tossing his rider. At the same time, Jonas dug his spurs into Rebel's ribs. Rebel jumped forward, crashing into Sandy Hair's gray. Sandy Hair screamed when his leg was crushed between the two horses. Jonas pulled him from the saddle, then both men fell, hitting the ground hard.

Will jumped from his horse, grabbed Sallow Face's shirtfront, and pulled him upright. Still holding the outlaw's shirt, he slammed three sharp jabs into Sallow Face's belly. He let the man loose, grabbing his right arm and twisting it hard as Sallow Face fell. The shoulder dislocated with an audible pop.

Jonas had landed on his back, with Sandy Hair on top of him. He head-butted the man, crushing his nose, blood spurting. He kneed Sandy Hair in the ribs, rolled him off, then slammed a punch

to the side of his jaw. Both outlaws lay unconscious.

"You all right, Jonas?" Will asked.

"Yeah. Just lost a little breath, is all. How about
you?"

"Just feel bad about hittin' that horse. I hated to
do that."

"I know. I'd feel the same if I'd had to."

Will removed the outlaws' gun belts, and
knives from each of them. He walked over to
Pete, lifted his canteen from the saddle horn, and
removed the cap. He poured some water over
both outlaw's faces, rousing them.

"What . . . the hell . . . happened?" Sallow Face
choked out.

"You two *hombres* picked on the wrong men,
that's what happened," Will said. "We're Texas
Rangers, assigned to clean up this territory.
Seems like we're off to a good start."

"What're you gonna do with us?" Sandy Hair
asked.

"I don't rightly know. First, gimme your
names."

"Blair Townsend," Sallow Face said. "My
pardner's York Temple."

"Mr. Temple asks a good question, Will," Jonas
said. "We can't take the time to haul their sorry
butts back to Sweetwater. But I don't reckon we
can just kill 'em, neither."

"No, I reckon we can't, although I'm sorely

150

tempted," Will said. "Tell you what. Pull off their boots. Get their rifles and canteens, too."

Jonas grinned.

"Sure thing."

He removed Temple's boots, then Townsend's.

"You ain't gonna leave us afoot, Ranger?" Temple cried.

"Yes and no. Jonas, tie those boots to their saddles."

"Yessir."

"You two listen up," Will said. "When we reach San Angelo, I'm gonna wire the sheriff in Sweetwater, to swear out arrest warrants. I won't have him execute those warrants, on one condition. You both ride out of Texas as fast as you can, and never come back. If either of you are found in this state again, you'll land behind bars. *Comprende*? I said, *comprende*?"

"Yeah. I reckon we do," Townsend said. He frowned.

"Good. There's a few more conditions. First, I'm confiscatin' your guns. Second, if you've got any friends in these parts, make certain they know the Rangers are gonna root every last lawbreaker out of this territory. Third, you tell nobody but the sheriff what happened. Anybody else asks, your horses got spooked, and threw both of you. Last, you'll start for Sweetwater by walkin'."

"You can't do that, Ranger," Temple protested.

151

"My ankle's swelled up like a balloon. It might be busted."

"And you pulled my shoulder clean out of its socket," Townsend said.

"I reckon you'll just have to lean on each other, then," Will answered. "You should be thankful I'm letting you keep your canteens. Jonas . . ."

Jonas handed Townsend and Temple their canteens.

"Now the horses, pardner."

Jonas pointed the outlaws' horses toward Sweetwater, then slapped them on their rumps. They took off at a run.

"All set, Will."

"Ranger, we can't make Sweetwater without horses," Temple said.

"You won't have to," Will answered. "They'll stop in a mile or so, probably at that creek up the road. You can pick 'em up there. If not, someone'll come along who can give you a ride. Either that, or me'n Jonas can plug the two of you right now, and be done with it."

"You're a Ranger. You wouldn't."

"Resisting arrest. I would. Now, we're headed south. If you intend to make town before dark, I'd suggest you get movin'. Unless you'd rather wait until the sun's down, when it'll be cooler. Of course, by then, someone'll have probably taken your horses."

Will nodded at Jonas, who pulled Temple to his feet, while Will stood Townsend up.

"Remember, don't stay in Texas any longer than it takes y'all to see a doc, and get patched up so you can ride," Will warned.

"Don't worry," Townsend answered. He scowled. "I don't ever want to see this god-forsaken hellhole again."

Will and Jonas mounted, then watched the two outlaws limp their way toward Sweetwater. Once the men were out of sight, they heeled their horses into a walk.

"You reckon they have any inkling we're not headed to San Angelo?" Jonas asked.

"Don't matter," Will said. "I reckon they won't ride to Sweetwater, anyway. I figure we put enough of a scare into 'em they'll keep on goin' until they're plumb out of Texas."

"About a mile or so ahead, the terrain gets lots more rugged for a ways, Jonas," Will said. It was about five in the afternoon. "Quite a few dry creek beds and washes, and the scrub gets real thick. We've got enough time to pass through that stretch before dusk. Soon as we do, we'll find a spot to spend the night."

"Sounds like that'd be a good place to make camp ourselves," Jonas answered. "We'd be pretty well hidden. Unlikely anyone'd spot us in that *brasada*."

"You're missing the point. I *want* anyone passin' by to know where we are. If it's an *hombre* bent on startin' trouble, like robbing or horse stealin', I want 'em to walk right into a trap. We'll sweeten the bait by havin' a good-sized fire tonight. That'll make us look like greenhorns. We'll be a real tempting target."

"Got ya. Boy howdy, I'm sure glad we picked up extra ammunition in Sweetwater. Seems like we're gonna need it."

"Let's hope not," Will answered. He'd no sooner said that when two shots rang out in the distance.

"You were sayin', Will? That sounds like more trouble."

"I wouldn't bet against it. Let's go."

They kicked their horses into a dead run. Half-a-mile on, they rounded a bend. A man was lying face down in the road. His horse was nearby, its reins tangled in the brush. A dust cloud from a dry wash indicated several horsemen were fleeing the scene.

"Check that man, Jonas," Will shouted. "I'll go after those *hombres*."

Jonas pulled up alongside the victim, took a quick look without even dismounting, then put Rebel into a run again, pounding up the draw right behind Will.

"There's two bullet holes in his back," he called to Will. "Nothin' we can do for him."

Leaning low over their horses' necks, the Rangers urged them on. They drew nearer to their quarry, now within earshot of the fleeing killers.

"We're gainin' on them," Will said. He pulled his rifle from its boot. Pete galloped around a bend and up a slight rise. Ahead, four men were whipping their horses, urging them up a steep trail out of the draw.

Will pulled Pete to a stop. The well-trained gelding stood stock while Will lifted his rifle, aimed at the foremost rider, and pulled the trigger. Will's bullet struck his target in the middle of the back. The man threw up his arms, and fell backwards over his horse's rump. The three men following had to swerve their horses to avoid trampling him. The lead horse stumbled and went down, the others tripping over it, spilling their riders. The men scrambled for cover behind a scattering of boulders. The horses regained their feet, reversed direction, and ran back toward Will and Jonas, apparently unhurt.

Will and Jonas dove from their saddles when the outlaws began firing back. Pete and Rebel followed the other mounts as they ran by to safety, out of gunshot range.

"They've got us pinned down, Will," Jonas called, from where he'd taken cover behind a fallen mesquite stump. On the opposite side from his partner, Will's only shelter was a slot in the wash's wall, which had been gouged out by floodwaters, sometime in the past.

"Mebbe, mebbe not," Will answered. "Appears like they've only got their pistols. We're pretty much out of six-gun range, and we've got our rifles. We should be able to pick 'em off."

"Um, Will. My Winchester's still on my horse," Jonas said.

"What! Dammit, Jonas."

"Sorry, Will."

"Tell that to them," Will answered, when an outlaw's bullet clipped the stump Jonas was behind, sending splinters in every direction.

"Hell, Will. I thought you said we're out of pistol range."

"I said 'almost out'. There's a helluva difference between 'almost' and 'all the way'."

Will took a snap shot, just to keep the outlaws in check. He ducked back, hugging the draw's wall when sand began spurting, as bullets hit all around him. He cursed, shot again, and an outlaw's hat flew off his head. The man ducked back behind a boulder.

"Jonas, I'm gonna try'n drive those men into the open," Will said. "If you get a chance to take a shot, do it."

Will went to one knee and began shooting, levering and firing his rifle as fast as he could, his bullets ricocheting off the rocks. One of the outlaws let out a yelp, then stumbled from behind a large boulder, went to his knees, and pitched to his face. Will looked at Jonas and shrugged.

"Must've been one wild ricochet."

While his partner reloaded, Jonas took his time with his shots, spreading them out until Will's rifle's cylinder was again full. He waved his six-gun at Will, then pointed, silently mouthing his intentions. Will nodded his understanding.

Jonas dropped to his belly behind the fallen log. He crawled to the draw's wall, crouched, and lunged up the slope. When he reached the top, he dove, rolled, and started shooting, the angle allowing him to ricochet his bullets into the last two outlaws' cover. The whining lead slugs drove them into the open, where Will dropped each with a bullet to the chest. He and Jonas waited for a moment. Detecting no movement from the downed men, they stood up, keeping their guns ready while they walked up to the downed men.

"Looks like you drilled this one right in the back, pard," Jonas said, examining the body of the man Will had shot from behind the rocks. "Nailed the other two plumb center."

"We were lucky," Will said. "Especially since you made a real rookie's mistake. You *always* grab your rifle when you're in a runnin' gunfight on horseback. It's a damn good thing those *hombres'* horses tossed 'em and ran off. If all three of 'em had gotten their hands on their rifles, it'd be us lyin' there with bullets in us, rather'n them."

"I know, Will, and I'm sorry. It was plumb stupid of me."

"It's over, so quit worryin' about it. Let's see what that dead *hombre* was carryin' that was worth these sons of bitches chancing a dry-gulchin' in clear daylight."

They checked the pockets of the three men, finding nothing but a few bills, some change, and cigarette makings.

"Nothing here. Let's see if the feller you shot off his horse has anythin' on him," Jonas said.

They walked back to where the body of the last outlaw lay. Will searched the rear pockets of the man's denims, then rolled him onto his back. The right breast pocket of his vest bulged. Will reached in and removed a large roll of hundred-dollar bills. It was held together by a gold money clip, engraved with the initials *"A.C."* Jonas whistled. "Whooee. That's a whole lot of *dinero*," he said.

"Sure is," Will agreed. "We'll count it later. For now, let's round up the horses. We'll go back and pick up the man they killed, and bring his body back here. We'll cover the bodies, then spend the night. We'll start back for Sweetwater at sunup."

"Change of plans?"

"Damn sure is. I don't want to chance anyone sneakin' up on us in the dark. We'll brush out all sign, as best we can, then roll out our blankets in these rocks. That'll keep us hidden until daylight. I doubt anyone honest takes this road after dark. No one should spot us, but we'll be ready, just in case."

Will whistled sharply. Pete trotted up to him, nuzzling his chest, begging for a treat. Rebel had followed him, and was lipping Jonas's left ear.

"You'll both get your treats in a bit," Will said. "We've got work to do first. Jonas, wait here while I round up those other broncs."

Will made quick work of catching the outlaws' horses, and driving them back to Jonas. Jonas tied them to a stunted redberry juniper, then mounted Rebel.

"Let's hope nobody happened by and discovered that dead *hombre*," Will said. "I'd hate to have 'em start shootin' before we could tell 'em we're Rangers."

They went back to the road. The murder victim was still lying where he'd fallen. A derby hat was alongside his head. Will untangled his horse, a tall blood bay mare, from the brush, and led it back to its rider. The horse snorted and shied at the scent of blood.

"C'mon, hoss. I don't have time for your foolishness, you jughead," Will scolded. When he brought the horse near the body again, it shied even more violently.

"She ain't gonna cooperate. Will," Jonas said.

"Toss that *hombre* up on Rebel, in front of me. He won't mind."

"You sure about that?" Will asked.

"Sure as I'm sittin' here. And we don't have time to fool with that damn hothead cayuse. We need to get off this road before someone sees us."

"All right."

Will lifted the body, and draped it over Rebel's withers. He broke a branch off a mesquite, and used it to wipe out most traces of the jumbled hoof prints, picked up the derby, then swung back into his saddle.

"Let's go."

They took the dead man back to where his killers' bodies still lay. His body was stretched out alongside the others. The man was dressed in a business suit. Will searched it for more evidence. He felt a bulge under the man's shirt. He unbuttoned the shirt's bottom two buttons, and removed a thick money belt, which was also lettered with the initials *"A.C.",* this time in gold leaf. Will opened the belt to reveal a thick sheaf of bills.

"Sees like those *hombres* were in too much of a hurry," he said. "There's plenty more money in this belt than what they found."

"More than we'll ever see in a lifetime as Rangers," Jonas said.

"Probably so," Will answered. "Wonder who this man was, and where he was headed with this much cash? He wasn't too smart, travelin' alone. Let's hope we can get some answers once we get back to town."

He stood up, and arched his back to remove a kink.

"Let's get the horses settled, so we can have our supper and grab some shut-eye."

He picked up Pete's reins, and the blood bay mare's.

"What the hell kind of saddle is that horse wearin'?" Jonas asked him. "I ain't never seen one like it. Bridle and bit are kinda funny-lookin', too."

"It's an Eastern saddle, or an English saddle. We generally call 'em kidney pads out here. Bridle's an English rig, too."

"The saddle don't look like it'd be much use."

"It's lighter on the horse's back, but you can't tie much to it, that's for damn certain," Will said. "Not any use for cattle work, or any hard work at all. This horse looks like somethin' from Kentucky or Tennessee, somewhere back East. I'd hazard her rider came from that way."

"He sure looks like a dude," Jonas said. "That would explain why he was stupid enough to carry that much cash through this territory. Was he even wearin' a gun? You didn't come up with one."

"He sure was."

Will pulled a revolver from inside the man's coat.

"Seems so. I haven't seen one of these in a long time."

"What is it?"

"It's a LeMat .36 caliber revolver. Nine shots, black powder, cap and ball. Used by the Confederate Army during the war. It's not the fastest firin' pistol, but it gets the job done, if a man knows how to use it. It's also got a nasty surprise, if you're not ready for it. See that second barrel?"

"Yeah."

"It's a smooth bore. Works as a short-barreled shotgun. The shooter flips this little lever to choose which barrel he wants. That's why his thing is also called the 'Grape Shot Revolver.' You don't want to see what it'll do to a man at close range."

"Not before supper, anyway," Jonas answered, chuckling. "Let's take care of the horses, then wrap these bodies up. I'd like to get this chore done. I'm plumb starved."

"Hope you don't mind jerky and hardtack then. We don't dare make a fire tonight. Not now."

"You're a mean man, Ranger Kirkpatrick. Real mean."

"Jonas, would you prefer the grub they serve at Huntsville?" Will asked.

"Now you've gone from mean to just plain cruel."

• • •

Will and Jonas arrived back in Sweetwater early the next afternoon. A crowd gathered, and followed them as they rode to the sheriff's office. Will told a young boy to run ahead and inform Butler of their return. The sheriff was waiting in front of his office when they rode up, along with Deputy Hawkins and Sweetwater Town Marshal Lincoln Tuttle.

"Seems you two have been busy," Butler said. He spat in the dirt.

"Just a tad," Will answered. "We came across four of these men, just after they'd killed and robbed the fifth. We ran 'em down, Seems they wanted no part of surrendering. We had to shoot it out with 'em."

"I reckon you won."

"I reckon. You mind takin' a look at these fellers and see if you recognize any of 'em, Sheriff?"

"Sure enough. I already know who owns that blood bay. He left town two days ago, headed for San Angelo. Lemme see if it's him."

Will had convinced the mare to carry her owner's body. Butler walked up to the horse, and lifted a corner of the blanket covering the corpse.

"Is it Chesterfield, Sheriff?" Tuttle asked.

"It is. Aubrey Chesterfield. I reckon the saloons and sportin' houses down in San Angelo just lost a good chunk of income. Reckon what we all knew what was gonna happen to him finally did."

"You mind explaining that, Sheriff?" Will asked.

"In my office, where we can talk in private. Soon as I look at the other corpses."

He went to the next body, and lifted the blanket.

"Mark Newton. Damn."

"That means two of the other ones are probably his brothers," Hawkins said. "But who the devil is the fourth one?"

"Can't tell if we don't take a look," Butler answered. He checked the next two bodies. "Yup. Josiah and Bobby. Let's take a gander at the last one."

When Butler looked at the final corpse, he stood, his mouth open in shock. He flushed bright red, then turned white as a ghost. He let loose a string of curse words, despite the ladies and kids present in the crowd.

"I take it you know him," Will said.

"Yeah. I sure do. This here's Jody, my big brother. I didn't even know he'd come back."

"We're sorry, Moe. Both of us," Will said. "We had no way of knowin'."

Butler lifted his voice.

"All right, folks. Show's over. Go on about your business. Anyone still here in five minutes, I'll have arrested for loitering. Linc, Paul, let's get these bodies down to Doc Pinkham. He'll need to write up coroner's reports."

He glared at Will and Jonas.

"You men better come along, too."

"I reckon we'd better," Will answered.

Butler slammed shut the door to his office.

"Sit down. You Rangers have some explaining to do. Two of those men were shot in the back. One of them was my brother."

"Just rein in a minute, Sheriff," Will said. "We'll answer all your questions, but we've got a few first. Soon as those are out of the way, we'll answer yours. Deal?"

Butler started to protest, then thought better of it. The authority of the Texas Rangers, and their actions, were pretty much unquestioned, and superseded that of any local law enforcement agencies.

"Deal."

With a long sigh, the sheriff settled back in his chair.

"I'll need a receipt for this *dinero* and other property I'm about to turn over to you. Three copies. I'll also need a sheet of paper and a pencil, *por favor*," Will said. "Jonas, take notes. They'll be the basis of our official report."

"Sure, Will."

Butler opened his top desk drawer, removed a sheet of paper, pencil, and eraser, along with three receipt forms. He handed them to Jonas, who touched the pencil to the brim of his hat.

"Much obliged, Sheriff."

"Let's get started."

Will took the stolen money out of his vest pocket, along with the money clip, and placed those on Butler's desk. He removed the money belt he had draped over his shoulder, and put that next to them, along with the LeMat revolver.

"There's one thousand, nine hundred and eighteen dollars in that stack," Will said. "Count it."

"No need. I trust you, Will."

"Moe, when it comes to stolen goods I'm turnin' over, I don't even trust myself," Will answered. "Count it."

"All right."

Butler took the bills and counted them.

"Nineteen hundred and eighteen dollars," he confirmed. "Soon as we're done here, I'll put it and the other items in my safe."

"Good. Once Jonas makes out the receipts, and we all sign 'em, we can move along."

It took Jonas a few minutes to fill out three receipts. When he was done, and everyone had signed the forms, Will gave one to Butler, and kept two for himself. One of those would be sent to Austin, along with his report.

"All right, that's set," he said. "Now to get the rest done. First thing, Moe. What can you tell me about the victim?"

"Aubrey Chesterfield? He showed up here

a few years back. Came over from London, England. Got money from back home once a month. Soon as he got it, he'd head down to San Angelo, just like clockwork. Threw most of it away on fancy women, drinkin', and gambling. He almost always came back purty near busted. Next month, once he got his money, he'd do it all over again."

"Remittance man," Will stated.

"So it seems," Butler agreed.

"What's a remittance man?" Jonas asked.

"The quick answer is a son from a family of British nobility, usually a black sheep of the family," Will explained. "You see, under the English law of primogeniture, the firstborn son inherits the entire estate. His brothers and sisters get nothing. Often, especially if a second or third son is causing scandal, the family will send him away, and forward him a monthly stipend . . ."

"Stipend?"

"Sum of cash to live on. Most remittance men are sent from England to Canada or Australia, since those countries are still under the British Crown. But quite a few end up out here, in the West."

"And most of 'em don't do much, except live off that money," Butler added.

"You're right, Moe. Some of 'em have started businesses, bought ranches, or found good jobs, but a lot of 'em still think, since they come from nobility, they shouldn't have to," Will said. "Quite often, the money they get from home is barely enough to scrape by. Sadly, on top of that, a lot of remittance men will blow through their allowance as soon as they receive it, then live hand to mouth until the next month. It seems like Chesterfield was one of those."

"He was," Butler confirmed. "Always came back from San Angelo with fancy new duds, but broke."

"He apparently wasn't too smart, either," Will said. "Everyone in these parts must've known his routine. I'm surprised he wasn't drygulched long before now."

"He most likely would've been, but he spread his money around here, too. Only reason he went to San Angelo was for a change of scenery. He'd take his time, usually took him three or four days to get there. And he was a dead shot with this here LeMat. A couple of drunk cowboys started in on him one night. They wouldn't quit. He was with one of the local soiled doves at the time. They kept tellin' him he wasn't a man, and didn't need no whore. One of those boys finally pulled a gun and told Chesterfield he was gonna plug him, if he didn't let them take the woman. Well, sir, Chesterfield just smiled, got real quiet, and pulled this here miniature cannon from under his coat. He shot both those men right between their legs. Dropped the two of 'em right there, howlin' and screamin' bloody murder. He smiled again, slid this gun back into his pocket, took the gal, and walked away. But not before tellin' those two they didn't need a woman, not no more."

"So he figured he could take care of himself," Will said.

"Which explains why he wasn't that far down the road when we found him," Jonas said. "He wasn't worried about anyone holdin' him up."

"That's right," Butler answered. "The only way anyone could've gotten the jump on that Limey was if they back shot him from ambush."

"It was only a matter of time before someone figured that out, and did," Will said. "Moe, what can you tell me about those men?"

"The Newton brothers were ne'er do wells. Their ma died givin' birth to Bobby. Their pa wasn't much account. He raised those boys on a small ranch just north of here. It was a hardscrabble place, barely provided enough food to keep those young'ns alive. Grogan Newton never did more'n a lick of work. He made some money doin' odd jobs, but spent more of it on liquor than on those boys. They started gettin' in trouble for petty thievin' before they even reached their teens. But it was always small stuff. Lotta folks felt sorry for the way they was brung up, so they didn't press charges, long as they got their stuff back. The Newtons spent some time behind bars, for drunk and disorderly, disturbin' the peace, saloon brawls, nothin' more'n that. I never figured those boys for cold-blooded murderers."

"That brings me to the hard question. I've gotta ask it. What about your brother?"

Butler's eyes misted. He swallowed hard before answering.

"Jody was my hero when we were growin' up. I followed him around like a puppy dog. When he turned eighteen, he got a job as a deputy sheriff for the county. I wanted to be just like him."

"What happened?"

"He got in a fight with Boyd Hartwell, whose family owned the biggest ranch in Nolan County. If they'd just stuck to usin' their fists, not much would've come of it. But Boyd pulled his gun. Jody shot and killed him. It was self-defense, but Hartwell's pa had the money and power to have Jody charged with murder."

"Was he convicted?"

"Yeah, but only on manslaughter, since everyone who saw the fight knew that Boyd started it, and a few of 'em stood up to Rance Hartwell, and testified to that. Still, Jody got sentenced to twenty years in Huntsville. But he never got there."

"Go ahead, Moe. I know this is hard. Take your time if need be."

"He escaped jail while waiting to be transported to Huntsville. It was a set-up. Two of Hartwell's men were waiting outside for Jody. They'd shot the sheriff, and killed him. Jody must've been suspicious, because he grabbed the sheriff's gun, and got Hartwell's men first. He disappeared. But two days later, the Hartwell ranch house burned to the ground. Killed the entire family. Everyone believes Jody did it. Last anyone saw of him was up in the Panhandle, lightin' a shuck for the Territories."

"Why do you think he came back?"

"*Quien sabe*? I've got no idea. But when he was a kid, he was friendly with the two oldest Newton brothers. If anyone'd know how to reach Jody, they would. I wouldn't put it past 'em to have sent him a message, offerin' him a chance for some easy money. I'm positive Jody was bitter enough he'd have taken it. All he ever wanted to be was a lawman, and that was taken from him by a greedy man, who ran roughshod over the entire county. Only good thing that came out of the whole affair was I decided to follow in Jody's boots. I swore Nolan County would have honest law. I promised that to Jody. And I've kept that promise."

"I'm sorry you had to go through all that. And really sorry we couldn't have brought your brother in alive."

"It's probably better you didn't Jody would have hung for certain. Least this way he died quick."

"Moe, that's pretty much all we needed to know. Go ahead and ask your questions, if you're ready."

"Won't ever be any readier, Will. First one is, not one of those men offered to give himself up?"

"I think you already know the answer to that one." Will said. "They knew Chesterfield was dead, and they'd be facin' a noose if they got caught. It was just their bad luck we came along when we did, or they probably would've gotten away with it. There were no witnesses, and I'm certain they would have gotten rid of the money clip. Long as they didn't start flashin' the money around, there'd have been no way to prove they killed Chesterfield."

"Here's the one that's botherin' me the most. Why were two of those men shot in the back?"

"Moe, it appears to me you've been a lawman long enough to realize a gunfight, especially on horseback, though the *malpais*, ain't all cut and dried. And it ain't pretty, neither. It's not like the dime novels, where the good guys always wait and let the bad guys take the first shot, the bad guys always miss, then the good guys cut 'em down. You know damn well that whenever someone is shootin' at you, you shoot back, and it don't matter whether your bullet takes 'em from the front or back, since they damn for certain don't care where they plug you."

"Is that what happened?"

172

"We had to stop them, any way we could, before they got away. We were down in a draw. They were already almost to the top of the trail out of it when we caught up with 'em. The only chance we had was droppin' the man in front. I tried for his horse, but it stumbled. My slug caught him in the back. It turned out to be your brother. The other three ducked into cover. We didn't have any. They had us pinned down. So I tried to drive 'em out into the open, by bouncin' a lot of bullets off the rocks behind 'em. One of the ricochets hit a Newton brother in the back. After that, Jonas flushed out the last two. They came out shootin'. I had no choice but to plug 'em. There's nothing more I can add."

"No, I guess not. You did what you had to. Look, I've got to make arrangements for my brother. Are you still planning on bein' on tomorrow's stage?"

"We are," Will said.

"I won't see you before the coach pulls out. The station agent is holdin' your tickets. If there's nothin' else, I need to head down to Doc Pinkham's. I want to take Jody to the undertaker myself."

"We understand, Moe," Will said. "We'll see you in a couple of days. Again, we're sorry."

"You were just doin' your jobs. I would've done the same, even if it was me facin' my own brother."

"Oh, I nearly forgot, Moe," Will said. "Did a couple of *hombres* come through town? One of 'em would have had his arm in a sling. The other had a busted nose, and would've been limpin' bad."

"As a matter of fact, they did. Asked for directions to Doc Pinkham's. Said their horses got spooked by a rattlesnake, threw 'em and run off. Claimed they had to walk almost two miles before they caught those broncs. I was goin' by doc's anyway, so I took 'em there. He wanted to keep them for a few days, until they healed up some, but they said they couldn't wait. Had to get to New Mexico Territory soon as they could. Any particular reason they wanted to vamoose so pronto?"

"Yup. They were chargin' travelers on the San Angelo road for protection. We showed them we didn't need any. Told those *hombres* to leave Texas for good. Warned 'em if they were still here when we got back we'd toss 'em in the calaboose."

"Well, they damn sure took your advice."

The hotel was fully occupied, so Will and Jonas arranged to sleep in the livery stable's hayloft. After saying good night to their horses, they climbed the ladder to the loft, spread out some loose hay, took off their boots, hats, and gun belts.

"Will," Jonas said, after they we lying on their blankets, on top of the hay. "I've gotta say somethin'."

"Get it off your chest."

"I know damn well you weren't aimin' for Jody's horse. You don't have it in you to hurt a horse, leastwise not on purpose. Neither do I, for that matter. You put that slug right where you aimed it, plumb center in Jody's back."

"I know, but Moe doesn't need to. His brother dyin' as an outlaw'll be hard enough on him," Will answered.

"You think he suspects?"

"Mebbe, mebbe not. I guess we'll never know for certain. Good night, Jonas. Go to sleep."

"G'night, Will."

11

Will and Jonas were at the Wells Fargo depot well before the stagecoach from Wichita Falls arrived the next morning. It pulled up about twenty minutes late. Several passengers got off, two of them women, who remained on the board-walk near the stage, evidently going to continue their journey. Two more men would board the stage here, in addition to the Rangers. While they waited for the hostler to change out the horses, the driver and guard loaded the new passengers' luggage. Will and Jonas only had their saddlebags and rifles.

"You two want those long guns up on top, or in the cabin with you?" the guard asked.

"Long as it's all right with you, we'd rather have 'em handy," Will answered. "Might be you'll need some extra guns. We've heard this trip is lousy with bandits."

"It can be," the guard answered. "You can stow them under the seat."

"*Gracias*. We're obliged."

Once all of the luggage was loaded, the driver gave a short speech.

"Listen up, all of you. My name's Gabe. My shotgun's is Hap. We've got five stops between here and San Angelo. Most of those will be just long enough to switch the horses. We'll stop for the night at Bronte, which is a little past the halfway point. We should get there between six and seven this evenin'. We don't travel at night on the next stretch of the route, because it's too dangerous. There's virtually no law for most of the way. If there's a holdup attempt, get down as low as you can. The walls of this here coach ain't thick enough to stop a bullet. Now, get aboard. We're already runnin' late. Probably can't make up the time, but we don't want to lose any more, neither. Any of you want to change your mind, do it now. Otherwise, climb on board."

The driver helped the two women back into the coach, allowing them to board first. Will and Jonas got in last, each taking a window spot on opposite sides of the cabin, Will on the left in the back seat, facing forward, Jonas on the right in the front seat, facing the rear. That way, they could see trouble approaching from any direction. With a yell from the driver, and a crack of his whip, the stage lumbered into motion.

"Are you certain you wouldn't prefer to sit by the window, ma'am?" Jonas asked the attractive young woman seated next to him. She was in her early twenties, with dark hair, light brown eyes, and a figure the conservative light green traveling dress she wore failed to conceal. "You'd get more air."

"No, but thank you, sir," she answered. "I've

found there's much less dust if I take the middle spot."

"You don't sound like you're from Texas," Jonas said.

The woman smiled.

"I'm not. I'm from Providence, Rhode Island. I've accepted a teaching position in San Angelo. My name is Pamela Smithers."

"I'm pleased to meet you, Miss Smithers. I'm Jonas Peterson. My pard is Will Kirkpatrick. We're on our way to look at some ranch land, outside of San Angelo."

"You're cowboys?"

"Yes, ma'am. Two of the toughest, hardest ridin' and hardest shootin' cowhands you'll ever run across."

"How thrilling to meet a genuine cowboy."

"My pardner's humble, too, as you can no doubt tell, Miss Smithers," Will said. "Welcome to Texas."

"Thank you, Mr. Kirkpatrick. Perhaps we should all become better acquainted. Would you mind telling us a little about yourself, sir?" she asked the man seated on her left. He was also in his early twenties, with red hair, green eyes, and a smattering of freckles across his nose and cheeks. He was dressed in a U. S. Army uniform, with corporal's stripes on its sleeves.

"Of course. My name's Sam Stoddard. As you undoubtedly noticed, I'm in the Army. I'm en

178

route to my new assignment at Fort Concho. I grew up in North Attleboro, Massachusetts."

"That means we're practically neighbors," Miss Smithers exclaimed. "Perhaps we'll be able to further our acquaintances."

"Perhaps we will," Stoddard said, smiling.

Will looked at Jonas, formed his right hand into a pistol, held it next to his hip, aimed it at Jonas, and fired the thumb trigger. He mouthed the words "shot down again", and chuckled. Jonas scowled.

"I'm Melissa Miller," the woman next to Will said. She was in her mid-fifties, with gray hair tied up in a severe bun. She was short, but not overly plump, just showing the weight most people gained as they grew older. "Miss Smithers and I met on the stage in Wichita Falls. I'm from Omaha, Nebraska. My husband passed away last year. My daughter and son-in-law insisted that I move down here to live with them. They seem to think I can't take care of myself. I decided to humor them, and come for an extended visit. I've rented out my home, in case I choose to go back to Omaha. My son-in-law runs a haberdashery in San Angelo. My daughter is due to have her first baby in three months. That's what finally convinced me to make the trip to this god-forsaken, dreadful place. The heat is horrible, and the land so parched and brown."

"Texas isn't all that bad, once you get to know

it," Will said. "Lots of people can hardly wait to move here and put down roots."

"What about you, sir?" Miss Smithers asked the man alongside Will. He was dressed in a cheap suit and tie, and wore a flat crowned hat. He was in his late thirties, brown haired and brown eyed. He was already sweating profusely. He took a handkerchief from his suit pocket and wiped his brow before answering.

"My name's Franklin Nelson, from St. Louis. I represent Zeller and Perkins, manufacturers of the finest knives and kitchen utensils in the country. My territory is all of Texas, so I spend most of my time traveling from place to place. My job has gotten a bit less stressful; however, with the railroads expanding so rapidly. Traveling by train is much faster and more efficient than by stagecoach."

The coach rattled and bumped over the rough, rutted road. Nelson complained when it jounced across a particularly deep chuckhole.

"Da—uh, darn this driver, and this road. Pardon my language, ladies. I'm just so tired of being bounced and bruised from one end to the other."

"Be grateful we're on this Concord coach, rather'n another make," Will said. "The leather thoroughbraces on Concords provide a much smoother ride than others. Not that it's easy to tell, I know."

"At least we're nearing the end of our journeys,

except for Mr. Nelson," Corporal Stoddard said. "Just one more day and night, then a few hours tomorrow."

"It will be a relief to finally reach our destination," Mrs. Miller said.

The passengers fell into light conversation, talking about family, the weather, and the countryside. Nelson opened his sample case, and convinced Miss Smithers to buy a set of knives, along with a potato masher, and a peeler. For the rest of the day, except for getting out to stretch their legs or relieve themselves at a stage station, they alternated between talking, looking out the windows at the passing landscape, or dozing. Will and Jonas checked with the agent at every station. Each assured them no highwaymen, or other sorts of suspicious men, had been seen. Horseback travelers, and freighters, who had passed by also informed the agents they had not been harassed. It was about six-thirty in the evening when they approached their overnight stopping place.

"Bronte! Comin' into Bronte!" Gabe yelled.

Most stagecoach drivers loved putting on a show when they drove into a town, and Gabe was no exception. He cracked the whip over his team, putting the six horses into a run. They galloped down Bronte's main street. When they reached the stage depot, he put on the brake and hauled back hard on the reins. The stage came to a sudden stop, enveloped in a swirl of dust. Mrs. Miller coughed, waving her hand in front of her face in a vain attempt to brush away the dust.

Gabe and Hap climbed down from the driver's seat, and opened the door for their passengers.

"The hotel's across the street," Gabe said, once everyone had alighted. "There's three restaurants on the same block. They're all decent. For you fellers, there's two saloons, this side of the street, three blocks down. Don't gamble in either of 'em. The games are crooked as a sidewinder. The town's usually pretty peaceable, but I wouldn't recommend you ladies go out unaccompanied after dark. You never can tell when some cowboy, who's in town from after a month or more on the range, gets himself too liquored up, and forgets his manners. That's puttin' it politely. It'd be better to get supper, then stay in your rooms until we're ready to leave in the mornin'."

"We appreciate your concern, and advice, driver," Mrs. Miller said.

The passengers' luggage was tossed down. The two women refused Jonas's and Corporal Stoddard's offer to carry their carpetbags to the hotel.

"C'mon, Jonas," Will said. "We might as well get ourselves settled for the night."

They shouldered their saddlebags. Carrying their rifles, they crossed the street to the Charlotte Hotel. A gray-haired woman in a blue gingham dress greeted them from behind the front desk.

"Good evening, gentlemen. Are you seeking accommodations for the evening?"

"Yes, ma'am. We sure are," Will answered.

"Excellent. I have one room left, if that's suitable. One dollar, in advance."

"It will be fine," Will answered. He took a silver dollar from his pocket and placed it on the desk. The clerk turned the register toward him.

"If you'll both sign, I'll give you your key."

Will and Jonas signed in turn. The clerk took a key from a pigeonhole behind the desk and handed it to Will.

"Room fifteen. Upstairs to the left. The room is the last one on the right. It's a corner room, so it's well ventilated if you open the windows."

"*Muchas gracias*, ma'am," Will said.

"Ma'am, before we go, I have to ask," Jonas said. "Is the hotel named after you? Are you Charlotte, the owner?"

"Heavens, no. I mean, yes, I own the hotel, but it's not named after me. My name is Harriet Dovetail. This town is named for Charlotte Bronte, the English novelist. Her sister was Emily Bronte, you may recall. But don't pronounce it 'Brahnt-tay,' as the family's name is pronounced. We just say 'Brahnt.' "

"Thank you, Miz Dovetail," Jonas said. "It'll be good to get some of this dust off, and sleep in a real bed tonight."

"You'll find a pitcher of water, basin, soap, and towels in your room, waiting for you."

"That sounds good, Miz Dovetail," Will said. "We're obliged."

He and Jonas went up to their room. As with most frontier hotels, it was sparsely furnished. There was a double bed, a chest which doubled as a washstand, and two straight backed chairs. On the chest were the promised pitcher, basin, soap, and towels. On the floor alongside it was a chamber pot.

"It ain't fancy, but at least it's clean," Will said. He hung his saddlebags over one of the chairs, and leaned his rifle against it. "Matter to you which side of the bed you take?"

"I'm not particular," Jonas answered. "It is a mite stuffy in here, though. If it's all the same to you, I'll take the side nearest the window."

He hung his gun belt on the other chair, then threw his hat on the bed.

"That's fine with me. Soon as we scrape some of the dust off our hides, we'll get supper, then mebbe swing by one of the saloons for a couple of beers."

"Maybe Miss Smithers will be having supper at the same time," Jonas said, his eyes brightening. "She sure is pretty."

"Jonas, it's plain as day she's got her cap set for that soldier boy."

"Only because she hasn't had the chance to get

to know me," Jonas answered. "She's probably just dazzled by his uniform. Wait'll she sees me all spruced up."

"You really think she'd want to marry an itchy-footed Texas Ranger, who'll leave her behind for weeks on end, while you chase owlhoots all over the state, her never knowin' whether or not you'll come home in a pine box. And before you say anythin', don't forget you're still on probation. You can't up and quit the outfit just because a pretty face turns your head."

"I suppose you're right," Jonas said. He shrugged. "Besides, an *hombre* like me don't have anythin' to offer a fine gal like that, anyway. You're right. I am itchy-footed. I damn for certain can't see myself settlin' down anytime soon."

"So there you have it. You gonna start washin' up? If not, I'm takin' first dibs on the soap'n water."

"All right. I can take a hint. Lemme just open the windows first."

Once he'd opened both windows, Jonas removed his shirt and neckerchief. He tossed them on the chair, then walked over to the chest to wash up. Will pulled a map out of his saddlebags, unfolded it, and spread it across the bed.

Will studied the map for a few minutes.

"Jonas, can you come over here, for just a minute?" he asked.

"Soon as I get the soap out of my eyes."

Jonas picked up a towel to rub the soap off his face. He draped it around his shoulders, then walked over to Will.

"What've you got?"

Will pointed to a spot on the map.

"You see this here. That's Poverty Canyon. It's the perfect spot for an ambush. If any robbers are gonna hit this stage, it'll most likely be there."

"How far from here?"

"About fifteen miles. It's close to five miles past a settlement called Tennyson."

"Another Texas town named after an English writer?"

"Seems so. Must've been a few Englishmen settled down in these parts."

Jonas looked more closely at the map. He pointed to another feature marked on it.

"What about here? This spot called Ignorant Hill. Looks like it might also be handy for a bunch of *hombres* intendin' to hold up a stage."

"You're right. I'm also lookin' at that one. I think Poverty Canyon'd be more likely because it's past the town. Hittin' a stage just before town would be takin' more of a chance."

"Unless they hit a northbound stage," Jonas pointed out.

"We'll have to keep that in mind on our way back," Will answered.

"Think we should warn the driver and shotgun?"

Will shook his head.

"I don't think we need to. They've been handlin' the run long enough they'll know all the likely holdup spots. We'll just have to be ready if trouble starts."

"You think we might get through to San Angelo without a holdup attempt?"

"What's your thoughts on that?"

"About as likely as my gelding sirin' a fine stud colt."

"So that's it. One thing we will have on our side, if an attempt is made at Poverty Canyon, is the horses will be fresh. The team'll be changed out at Tennyson. That might give us a chance to outrun any holdup men, if it comes to that."

"Not very likely. They'll have fresh horses, too."

"You're learnin', pard. Listen, finish washin' up, then I'll clean myself off, and we'll get our supper. We can still stop for a couple of drinks after that, but I don't want to stay out too late. We'd better clean our guns before we turn in."

"That makes sense. I'm just about finished. Just have to towel off. I'll knock some of the dust off my clothes and boots, while you wash. Dunno about you, but I'm hungry,"

"I could stand a bite," Will said.

After their meal, Will and Jonas stopped at the Texas Plains Saloon to have a couple of beers.

187

They were on the way back to their hotel when they heard several people arguing.

"That sounds like the ladies from the stage, Will," Jonas said. "Think we should find out what's goin' on?"

"You're damn right we should," Will answered.

They hurried their pace. A block-and-a-half later, they came upon Melissa Miller and Pamela Smithers. A cowboy held Miss Smithers around her waist. A second was trying to hold back Mrs. Miller, who was swatting at him with her beaded reticule.

"Quit fightin' me, darlin'," the cowboy holding Miss Smithers said. "We're just gonna have a little fun, you'n me."

"Unhand me, you brute," Miss Smithers said. "You have no right to be manhandling me like this."

"You heard the lady. Let her go." Will ordered. He wrapped his hand around the butt of his six-gun.

"And you get your hands off the other woman," Jonas told the second man.

"This ain't none of your business," the man holding Miss Smithers answered. "Me'n this here fine-lookin' filly are just gonna have us a little fun. Ain't that right, sweet thing?"

"Texas Ranger. I'm makin' it my business," Will retorted. "Let go of the lady, now!"

Instead, the man jerked out his pistol and

pressed its barrel to the side of Miss Smithers's head.

"She's comin' with me. If you try'n stop me, I'll put a bullet through her brain. Then I'll gut-shoot you."

"You gone plumb loco, Billy?" his partner said. He had stopped fighting Mrs. Miller, and had his hands raised shoulder high.

"I mean it, Ranger. Either you or your pardner pulls a gun, and this woman's dead. Unbuckle your gun belts and let 'em fall. Your pard first."

Neither Will nor Jonas could take a chance on hitting Miss Smithers instead of Billy.

"All right. Just don't hurt her," Will said. "Go ahead, Jonas. Drop your gun belt."

"You won't get away with this, mister," Jonas said. He hesitated, then unbuckled his belt.

"Now you."

Will started to unbuckle his belt. With his gaze on the Rangers, Billy didn't notice Miss Smithers reach into the folds of her skirt. Without warning, he screamed, then stumbled back, blood flowing from a gash in his left leg, darkening his pants leg.

"Damn you, bitch!"

He tried to lift his gun to shoot Miss Smithers. Will drew his Colt and shot him in the chest. Mrs. Miller swooned, while Miss Smithers stood unfazed, gazing at the dying cowboy. She held a long-bladed kitchen knife in her right hand.

Blood glistened scarlet on the blade. She turned to Will and Jonas.

"Mr. Nelson wasn't exaggerating. This *is* the sharpest knife I've ever handled. It has a nice balance, too."

A small crowd had gathered. Will looked at the nearest man.

"This town got a marshal?"

"Marshal? Hell, Ranger, we ain't even got a jail. Pardon my language, ladies."

Will glared at Billy's partner.

"You got a name? I want his, too. What part did you play in this?"

"Rufus Cannon. His was Billy Hewitt. I just wanted to kiss that lady there. Billy dared me to try, after he said he was gonna kiss the other one."

He pointed to Mrs. Miller, who had revived, and was sitting up.

"Ruffian!" she said to Cannon.

"You weren't intendin' to do worse, like your pard was?"

"No, sir, Ranger. I swear. Billy must've let the whiskey get to him. That happened a lot with him."

"Did this man hurt you, Mrs. Miller?" Will asked.

"I don't believe as badly as I hurt him."

Cannon had a large lump rising on his jaw, along with a swollen and blackened left eye.

Blood trickled from his smashed lips. Mrs. Miller was evidently deadly with her beaded reticule.

"So it seems," Will said. He chuckled.

"Mrs. Miller, since Tennyson has no jail, or law, if you press charges, I'll have to arrest this man. That means I'd have to haul him with us on the stage, until we reach San Angelo. Now, if you decide you want to see him arrested, I'll understand. However, it seems to me he's been punished enough, between you pounding the dickens out of him, and his pard dead. Even worse—or I guess I should say, 'better,' you humiliated him by givin' him a public beating."

"No, I certainly don't want him on the stage with us," Mrs. Miller replied. "Sir, you may go. Depart, and never let me see you again."

"Ranger, you mind if I take Billy with me, and bury him at the Q Bar Q? That's the ranch where we both worked."

"Any of the other hands gonna come lookin' for us?"

"No, Billy wasn't well-liked. He had a temper. Only reason I was with him is the boss asked me to ride herd on him. He won't be too pleased about what happened, but he won't be surprised, neither. Once Billy got riled up, nobody could handle him."

"All right. One of you men give him a hand loadin' his pardner on his horse. The rest of you, go on about your business," Will ordered. "Miss

Smithers, me'n Jonas are escorting you and Mrs. Miller back to the hotel, now. The stage driver warned you it wouldn't be safe to go out after dark."

"I know we shouldn't have, but our room was so stuffy. We just had to get out to take a constitutional, and get some air."

"You nearly got a lot more than you bargained for," Will said. "Let's go."

Miss Smithers walked alongside Jonas.

"Thank you for coming to our rescue," she said.

"Aw, t'warn't nothin'," Jonas said. He blushed. "You were mighty brave, standin' up to that *hombre*."

"Truthfully, I was terribly frightened. I'm certainly glad I decided to tuck that knife into my skirt. I know he would have killed me, once he—"

"You don't need to say any more," Jonas said.

They walked in silence the rest of the way. When they got to the hotel, Miss Smithers gave Jonas a quick peck on the cheek, then ran inside before he could say anything.

"Dang," Will said.

"Yeah, dang," Jonas repeated, rubbing his cheek.

12

The next morning, after leaving Tennyson, the stage rolled steadily onward toward its final destination, San Angelo. While it wasn't apparent to their fellow travelers, Will and Jonas grew more alert as it neared Poverty Canyon. When it reached the canyon's mouth, seven masked men on horseback, guns in hand, emerged from the brush. Two of them shot into the air, while two of the others cut off the coach. Gabe hauled back on the reins, bringing the stage to a stop. One of the holdup men grabbed the leaders' harnesses. The others circled the stage.

"Listen up!" the apparent leader shouted. "Do what we say, and no one gets hurt. First, driver, you'll throw down the strongbox. Then, everyone inside will get out, and hand over your valuables. Try'n hide anything, and you'll get a bullet for your trouble. No sudden moves."

Will put a finger to his mouth to warn the other passengers to keep quiet, as he and Jonas eased their pistols out of their holsters. Corporal Stoddard unsnapped the flap of his holster, and slid out his pistol. He shifted, to cover Miss Smithers from any bullets.

"Two on each side, and three in front," Will whispered to Jonas. "If we can take out the four, that should cause enough confusion to give the guard and driver enough time to get the front three. You ready?"

Jonas nodded.

"On three. One, two, three."

Will put the barrel of his six-gun against the thin wood paneling of the coach, tilted it upward slightly, and aimed at the man nearest him. He shot right through the paneling, his bullet taking the robber in his belly, then angling up into a lung. Before his partner had time to react, Will stuck his gun out the window, and shot him in the chest.

At the same time, Jonas spun around in his seat, took out one of the robbers on his side with a bullet in the stomach. The second man got off a quick shot, which punched through the window frame, just above Jonas's head. He returned fire, hitting the man in the leg. The holdup man shot again, his bullet ripping into Corporal Stoddard's right side, at the same time Stoddard pulled his trigger. His shot hit the man in his throat, severing his jugular.

Curses came from the three robbers at the front of the stage, quickly cut off when the guard fired one barrel of his shotgun into the man on the left, then swung and put the second barrel's load of buckshot into his partner. The third man, panicked, spun his horse to flee. The driver pulled out his pistol and put two bullets into the man's back.

"You folks inside all right?" Gabe called, from his seat.

"Everyone but the corporal," Will answered. "He caught a slug. Don't know yet how bad he's hurt."

"I'll . . . be fine," Stoddard gasped. "Just got me . . . in my . . . ribs."

"Ladies, stay in here, while we take care of things outside," Will ordered.

"Of course. We'll tend to the corporal's wound," Mrs. Miller said.

"You can't," Stoddard objected. "Wouldn't . . . be decent to take my shirt off . . . in front of . . . you ladies."

"Nonsense. It would be far more indecent if you bled to death in front of us," Mrs. Miller retorted.

"I'll see if the driver has a medical kit," Nelson offered.

"If he doesn't, we can use our petticoats for bandages," Mrs. Miller said.

Will and Jonas, guns still in their hands, got out of the stage. Gabe had just stepped down from his seat. Hap was checking the bodies of the two men he'd shot, along with the one Gabe had killed.

"These three are all goners," he said. "That was quick thinkin' on you fellers' part. How'd you know there'd be a robbery attempt here?"

"We didn't, for certain; but it seemed like the

195

most logical spot," Will answered. He examined the bodies of the men he'd shot. Both were dead. On the other side of the coach, Jonas checked the last two robbers. The one he and Stoddard had shot was dead. His neck was so thickly coated with blood it appeared he was wearing a scarlet neckerchief. The man Jonas had shot in the stomach was unconscious, but still breathing. From the amount of blood spreading over his shirtfront, it was obvious he'd received a fatal wound.

Gabe eyed Will and Jonas narrowly.

"Who are you fellers, anyway? You dang sure ain't just two cowboys, lookin' to buy a ranch."

"No, we're not," Will admitted. "I'm Will Kirkpatrick. This here's my ridin' pard, Jonas Peterson. We're Texas Rangers, assigned to clean out the renegades plaguin' this territory."

Will was one of the few Rangers who actually wore a badge, the preferred silver star in silver circle design. He usually kept it concealed in his vest pocket. Now, he took it out, showed it to the driver, then slipped it back into his pocket.

"Well, you're off to a good start. Although you look to be a mite young for a Ranger, sonny," Gabe said to Jonas.

"And you look a tad long in the tooth to still be handlin' a stage for Wells Fargo," Jonas shot back. "As far as my age, I'm old enough."

Gabe turned his attention back to Will.

"Wells Fargo ain't gonna be too happy about the hole you blasted through their stagecoach, Ranger."

"They'd be a lot less happy if we'd let those *hombres* rob the coach, and probably kill at least some of us," Will answered.

"Gabe, quit your usual nonstop jabberin'," Hap said. "Let's clean up this mess so we can get rollin'. Easiest thing to do is lay these dead *hombres* across their horses, then tie the animals to the back of the stage and take 'em into town. You agree with me, Rangers?"

"Yep," Will said. "We've also got to get the soldier to a doc quick as we can. Haven't had the chance to check his wound yet, but he was losin' quite a lot of blood. Sooner we get movin', the better."

The outlaws' horses were gathered, their riders' bodies lashed over their saddles. Once the horses were tied together, and tethered to the back of the stage, Will and Jonas started to climb back inside. Corporal Stoddard was lying across the front seat. Strips of blood-soaked petticoats were wrapped around his middle as makeshift bandages. His head was in Miss Smithers's lap. She was using a lace handkerchief to wipe sweat off his brow.

"How bad off is he?" Will asked.

"I can't say for certain," Nelson answered. "The bullet's still in him. He's lost a lot of blood, but I think we've managed to stop the flow. We can't waste any time getting him to a doctor."

"I'll ride up top," Will said. "Jonas, you give these folks a hand with the corporal."

"Right," Jonas said.

"Tell the driver to hurry, Ranger," Miss Smithers pleaded. "We can't let Corporal Stoddard die. Not after he was so brave, and saved my life. The bullet which struck him would have hit me, if he hadn't protected me."

"I will."

Will clambered into the driver's bench, and settled alongside the guard. Gabe slapped the reins on the team, and cracked his whip over their head, putting them into a gallop.

Yet again, Will and Jonas had to explain to the local authorities what had happened, try to identify the dead men, and telegraph a brief report to Austin. After writing up a full report and leaving it at the hotel's front desk for mailing, they had supper, and a couple of beers at the nearest saloon. They were standing out front, smoking.

"Jonas, you want to call it a night?"

"I dunno, Will. I guess we should. But what I'd really like to do is get rip-snortin' drunk."

"You're still pinin' over that gal, ain't you?"

"I guess. Dammit, I thought I might have a chance with her. Then that soldier boy goes and gets himself shot. Now he's her hero. Bet'cha she stays with him day'n night until he's all healed up. Then she'll marry him."

"Jonas, let me give you a piece of advice. No gal is worth takin' a bullet for. Especially if that bullet leaves you dead."

"I know, Will. But doggone it."

"Tell you what, pard. I know how to make you feel better. We'll go over to Miss Hattie's."

"Miss Hattie's? What's that?"

"Miss Hattie's is the fanciest bordello in San Angelo. She's got some real fine gals workin' for her. Spending some time with one of them will perk you right up. What d'ya say?"

"Why not?" Jonas said, with a shrug. "I could use a little female company."

13

The only passengers on the return stage to Sweetwater were Will and Jonas. They reached Tennyson without incident, where the stop was just long enough to switch out the horses.

"Ignorant Hill's comin' up soon," Jonas said, shortly after the trip resumed. "If there's gonna be trouble, it'll happen there."

"I dunno," Will answered. "The hill is pretty far off the trail, three or four miles to the east. That'd be quite a run for anyone attemptin' to ambush this stage."

"Yeah, but there's plenty of brush for an hombre to use for cover," Jonas pointed out. "And once they make that hill, they'll have the high ground. They'll be able to duck into cover, and pick off anyone pursuing 'em, real easy."

"You make a strong case," Will answered. "I reckon we'll know soon enough."

The stage raced by the rough trail which led to ignorant hill. Once it was past, six riders burst out of the brush, firing their guns while they chased after the coach.

"Seems like you were right, Jonas," Will shouted. "We're gonna have our hands full." He grabbed his rifle from where it lay on the seat next to him. He and Jonas added their gunshots to those of the shotgun guard. The driver slapped his reins on the team, yelling at them with a string of curses. The horses, rested and eager, broke into a dead run.

"At least we've got fresh horses," Jonas said. "With any luck, mebbe we'll be able to outrun these here sons of bitches."

"I doubt it," Will said. He sent another bullet at their pursuers. "They seem to be gainin' on us already. And I'm certain Gabe is gettin' everything out of the team he can."

The stage rocked and jounced over the rough road. Accurate aim was impossible, both for its passengers and the would-be holdup men. Will steadied his rifle on the window fame, aimed, and fired at the nearest rider. Luck was with him. The slug took the man in the center of his chest. He sloughed sideways off his horse.

"You got him," Jonas exclaimed. "That's one less."

"That still leaves five more," Will said.

Hap, the guard, had turned and knelt in his seat, shooting over the coach's roof at the oncoming gang. After emptying his Greener, then reloading, he lifted up to shoot again, only to take a bullet in his chest. He cried out when another slug struck him, and started to pitch off the stage. Gabe grabbed him by his shirt and pulled him back. Hap slumped into the driver's boot, unconscious, or dead.

"Sounds like they got the guard," Jonas said.

"Yup," Will answered. He ducked when a bullet splintered the window frame just above his head. "They're gettin' within pistol range, too."

The stage was rounding a bend, nearly tipping over, when one of the outlaws put a bullet into Gabe's back. He sagged forward, dropping the lines. The team, with no one handling the reins, panicked at all the gunfire, put on a fresh burst of speed.

"They got the driver, too!" Jonas yelled. "We're on a runaway. I'm gonna try'n get to the driver's seat. Mebbe I'll be able to reach the reins and bring those horses under control."

"No, don't try it," Will said. "You'll either get shot, or tossed off the coach. Those renegades are closing in, fast. I've got an idea. It's a long shot, but it just might work. Those *hombres*'ll stop the horses for us, if it does. Don't have time to explain it. Just follow my lead. I hope you're a good actor."

Will leaned out the window as far as he dared, then emptied his rifle at the oncoming outlaws. He yelped, then slumped over the windowsill. He dropped his Winchester to the road. The wind ripped Will's hat off his head as it buffeted his body.

"No! Will!" Jonas screamed. The five remaining outlaws were almost alongside the coach now. Jonas fired three last shots, hitting one in the shoulder. The outlaws returned his fire, several bullets hitting the coach, some of them puncturing the side panels. Jonas jerked, yelled, and fell back against the seat, his right arm hanging out the window. His head hung limply on his shoulders.

"Silas. You'n Bret stop those horses," the gang's leader ordered. One on each side, the chosen pair urged their horses alongside the stagecoach's team. They leaned over in their saddles, grabbed the lead horses' harnesses, and pulled them to a stop.

"Make certain everybody's dead," the leader ordered. "Soon as we're finished here, we'll have to pick up Trace. Jackson, how bad are you hit?"

"Not bad. I'll be all right until we're outta here."

Jonas began moaning. He slid lower in the seat.

"Muh . . . muh belly. I got plugged . . . in the gut. Damn . . . Feels like . . . someone's runnin' . . . a hot poker . . . through muh . . . guts. Hurts . . . somethin' awful. Someone help . . . me. Please . . . help . . . me."

"Sounds like one's still alive, Mike. And he wants help."

"Seems to be, Dale," Mike, the leader, agreed.

"You reckon we should help the poor bastard, by puttin' him out of his misery?"

"Like you said, he's askin' for help. It'd be right charitable. Go ahead."

203

Dale grinned in anticipation.

"This'll be a pure pleasure."

He dismounted, walked up to the stage, and opened the door. Left-handed, Jonas shot him in the belly. Dale jackknifed, and fell backward to the dirt.

"You damned son of a bitch!" he cursed.

Before Mike had a chance to react, Jonas, still using his left hand, shot him off his horse. Jackson, the man Jonas had wounded, shot Jonas in the left side. Will slid back into the cabin, and pulled out his pistol.

The two men who had stopped the runaway team heard the gunshots, and saw their partners go down. Will shot the man on his side of the coach, then fired over the roof of the stage, first downing Jackson, then drilling the last robber through his forehead. After the final shot echoed away, the only sounds were the nickering and stamping of the nervous horses, and the groans of the wounded robbers.

"How bad you hit, Jonas?" Will asked.

"I'm not certain. Bullet's still in me."

"Can you last until I make certain of these hombres?"

"Damn sure can. I'll help you."

"You sure?"

"I am."

"All right. Let me give you a hand outta there."

Will helped Jonas down from the coach. He

looked at the blood spreading across the left side of Jonas's shirt.

"You might want to take off your neckerchief and stuff it inside your shirt, to try'n slow the blood," he suggested. "It looks like you're bleedin' pretty good."

"I reckon you're right."

Jonas pulled the wild rag from around his neck, folded it, and placed it over the wound.

Two of the outlaws were still clinging to life: Dale, the man who'd intended to finish off Jonas, and taken a bullet in his gut from Jonas for his trouble, and Mike, the leader. They were lying near each other. Will and Jonas kicked their guns away.

"Damn you to Hell," Dale said, when he saw Jonas. "Thought . . . you'd been gut-shot. I was . . . gonna finish you off."

"Thought you . . . were done for . . . too," Mike said to Will, who recognized him.

"Mike Hardy. The Rangers have been lookin' for you and your gang for a long time. You boys were pretty stupid," Will said. "The only robbers who chase stagecoaches are in dime novels. If you'd known what you were doin', you would have come out of the brush in front of the stage, and stopped it."

"Way . . . we've always . . . pulled off . . . our robberies. Chase down . . . the stage, plug the driver and guard . . . from behind."

"Then you've been lucky, up 'til now. Seems like your luck finally ran out. Me'n my pard are Rangers."

"I reckon . . . your pard's luck . . . ran out, too, Ranger," Dale choked out. "Looks like I did . . . plug him. He'll bleed out . . . before he gets . . . to a doc."

"I wouldn't count on that," Jonas said.

"I'll see you in Hell, Ranger."

Dale grabbed his belly, rolled onto his side, and vomited up blood. His breathing ceased.

"Not for a while," Jonas muttered. Under his breath he added, "At least, I hope not."

"All the rest of your men are goners, Hardy," Will said. "You ain't got long, neither. You got anythin' to say before you meet your Maker?"

Jonas's bullet had ripped through the outlaw leader's right lung. Pink froth bubbled out of his mouth and nose with each tortured breath.

"Nope. Not to you, anyway."

Hardy gave a long sigh. His body shuddered, then went slack.

"Jonas, we'd better check the driver and guard, just in case," Will said. "After we load these *hombres* into the coach, we'll go back to the relay station at Tennyson."

Will climbed to the driver's seat. Both Gabe and Hap had been killed by outlaw bullets, the bullet which stuck Gabe severing his spine. Hap had taken both slugs in his chest. Will dragged them from the seat to the roof of the stage, and lashed their bodies in place.

"Lemme check you, before we load up the others," he told Jonas. "Get inside the coach, where you'll be out of the sun."

"Sure, Will."

Jonas climbed back in the stage, and sat down. He was sweating profusely, his skin was turning pale.

"I'm gonna take a look, and see how bad you're hit," Will said.

"All right."

Will opened Jonas's shirt, and pulled the neckerchief away from the wound. Blood still oozed from the hole in Jonas's side.

"Damn," Will said.

"What?"

"You're right. The slug's still in you somewhere. I was hopin' it was just a deep graze."

"Can you dig it out?"

Will shook his head.

"Uh-uh. It's in too deep. Best I can do is bind that wound up to try'n stop the bleedin'. Soon as that's done, we'll toss the bodies in here, and head back to the station. Think you'll make it that far?"

"I know I'll make it that far. And before you even suggest it, I damn sure ain't ridin' in here with six dead men. I'll ride up top, with you."

"Long as you can make it up to the seat."

"You can bet your hat I'll make it up to the seat."

"*Bueno.*"

Will removed Jonas's shirt. He tore off the sleeves, folded the shirt into a square, placed that over the bullet hole in Jonas's side, then tied the sleeves together and wrapped them around Jonas's middle, knotting them over the makeshift bandage to hold it in place.

"You take it easy while I gather the bodies, and round up the horses," he ordered Jonas.

"No." Jonas shook his head. "I'll be better off if I give you a hand. That'll get the job done quicker, and us back to town sooner. This bullet needs to come out soon as possible."

"I don't like the idea, but I ain't gonna take the time to argue with you," Will answered. "Let's get this chore done."

The bodies of Mike Hardy and the four of his men who had died in Will's trap were loaded into the stage. Their horses were strung together, and tied to the back of the coach. Will helped Jonas into the driver's seat, then picked up the reins and turned the stage around. They stopped to retrieve Will's hat and Winchester, and pick up Trace, the man Will had killed during the chase, and his horse. Once that was done, Will clucked to the team, putting them into a fast trot.

• • •

It was less than five miles from the site of the attempted hold-up to the Tennyson relay station. Will arrived there in less than fifteen minutes. Charlie Waters, the station agent, heard the stage as it approached. He, along with his twenty-year-old son, Eddie, were waiting in the yard when Will pulled up.

"What the hell happened, Ranger?" he shouted.

"Holdup. We got all of the sons of bitches, but they killed both the driver and shotgun. Shot my pardner, too."

"I can see that," Waters said. "How bad is it, son?"

"Dunno for certain," Jonas answered. "Lost a lotta blood. Gettin' kinda light-headed, too."

"And the slug's still in him," Will concluded.

"Let's get him inside, so we can take a look at him," Waters said. "Eddie, you'll have to change teams, then run this coach and the bodies into San Angelo. The agent in town's gonna have to send a message to Sweetwater, lettin' 'em know they've got to send down a replacement driver and guard on the next outbound stage."

"Right, Pa."

"I'll be goin' with you," Will said. "Jonas needs to get to a doc soon as possible. I've also got to advise the sheriff what happened, and send a report to Austin."

"Sure, Ranger."

Jonas was now semi-conscious, groaning with pain and babbling incoherently.

"Beggin' your pardon, Ranger, but that boy won't live to make town, from what I see," Waters said. "Looks like he's still bleedin'. We'd better let my wife take a look at him."

"Mebbe you're right," Will conceded. "C'mon, Jonas, let's see what we can do for you."

Waters and his son helped Jonas down, with Will following.

"Eddie, me'n the Ranger will take him from here. Go tell your ma we're bringin' her a wounded man that needs tendin'."

"On my way."

Eddie hurried inside the station. Will and Waters draped Jonas's arms over their shoulders, supporting him as he half-walked, half-stumbled. Mrs. Waters was waiting at the door, along with Eddie.

"Where do you want him, Louise?" her husband asked.

"Let me cover the back table with a sheet. I'll work on him there. Josie is already starting water to boil."

Jonas was unconscious now, only kept upright by Will and Waters. Mrs. Waters hurriedly spread a clean sheet over the table.

"I'm ready."

Jonas was laid on the table, placed on his back.

"You take it easy, pard," Will said to him, not

certain if Jonas heard. "I'm takin' one of the outlaw's horses, and ridin' for San Angelo to fetch a doctor. Be back with one quick as I can. Don't you quit on me, y'hear?"

"This boy won't last long enough for you to bring the doc from town, Ranger," Mrs. Waters said. "He's got one chance. That's if I can get the bullet out of him."

Will hesitated before answering. He shook his head.

"I dunno. I looked at his wound back at the ambush site. The bullet's in awful deep, so deep that I won't attempt to dig it out. No disrespect, Mrs. Waters, but do you really think *you* can?"

"Ranger, me'n Charlie have been out here since the Comanch' and Kiowas were still runnin' loose, raidin' all over this territory. Fought them, and Mexicans roamin' the land, too. Now it's white renegades we have to deal with. We've been workin' for Wells Fargo for nigh onto fifteen years, runnin' this station for more'n ten. I've dug out more bullets than most medicos see in a lifetime. I've pulled out arrows, fixed knife wounds, and once sewed up a belly wound from a Comanche warrior's lance. Had to stitch up the poor *hombre*'s guts, but he lived. I've set broken bones, treated cuts, sprains and snakebites, even delivered a few babies. Now, if you'd rather chance this poor boy bleedin' out before you make it to town, you go right ahead and take him. But if you want to give him any chance at all, let me get to work on him. And I mean right now, before he's lost any more blood, and it's too late."

"All right, Mrs. Waters. Go ahead. Do everything you can for him."

"You have my word, Ranger."

"Pa, if you'n Ma don't need me, I'd best run the stage into town. I'd rather get there before dark," Eddie said.

"You go ahead," Waters answered. "Your ma and sister shouldn't need any help. If they do, I'll be here with 'em. You might as well spend the night in San Angelo. It'll be safer than travelin' after dark."

"*Bueno*. I'm on my way."

"Charlie, get my big pan from the cabinet. Also, the things I use for cuttin' on a person. And a full bottle of whiskey."

"Right away."

"Mrs. Waters, is there anythin' I can do to help?" Will asked.

"Simply stay out of my way. You can watch if you'd like."

"*Gracias*."

Mrs. Waters opened Jonas's shirt, then removed the makeshift bandage.

"This is gonna be a tough one," she said. "Josie! Is that water ready?"

"I'm just bringin' it, Ma," a young girl

212

answered. A moment later, she came from the kitchen, carrying a stack of towels, a metal basin, and a kettle of steaming hot water. Right behind her was her father, holding a large pan containing knives and other instruments, plus an unopened bottle of whiskey.

"Josie, bring that water over here. Charlie, soak those instruments in whiskey while I clean out this fella's wound."

She turned to glare at Will.

"How the hell can the damn Rangers let a boy this young join up, only to get himself shot, just maybe shot dead? You needn't act so shocked at my cussin', neither, Ranger. It ain't nothin' I don't hear all the time, runnin' a relay station."

"He's eighteen," Will answered.

"Still too damn young."

Mrs. Waters soaked a towel in hot water, then used it to wipe blood and dirt from Jonas's side. Jonas stirred, and awakened.

"Where . . . where am . . . I?"

"Hush now, son, and keep still," Mrs. Waters ordered. "You're back at the relay station in Tennyson. You've been hurt bad. There's a bullet deep in your side. I've got to dig it out. We can't wait for a doctor. You'd die before one could get here. Do you understand?"

"I . . . reckon. But are you . . . sure I ain't . . . in Heaven? That purely does look like . . . an angel . . . standin' alongside you."

213

Josie smiled and blushed.

"That's Josie, my daughter. I'm Louise. She's gonna help me. And now ain't the time for you to be thinking about young ladies. You listen to me. I can see where the bullet went in, between two of your ribs. It's gonna be a devil of a job to get it out, without tearin' up your guts. I just hope and pray it didn't hit any of your vitals."

"Feels like . . . fire."

"I'm sure it does. Now, you pay attention. I'm gonna have to pour whiskey into that wound before I start pokin' around your innards. Then, I've got to probe for the bullet, and hope to God it's where I can get at it, *and* pull it out. If you think you hurt now, when I start diggin' for that slug, it's gonna feel like I'm sticking a hot sword between your ribs. With luck, you'll pass out again. If you don't, you'll need to hold as still as you possibly can. I'll give you a rag to bite down on. That'll help some with the pain. My husband and your pardner'll be holding you down. If you move at the wrong time, it could very well be the death of you. Let me know if you don't want me to try this."

"If you don't, I'm . . . done for, right?"

"Right."

"Reckon there's . . . no choice."

"Good boy. I've got to finish cleaning away the dried blood, then I'll get started. Josie, hand me another towel. You might want to soak one in cold water, and hold it on this boy's forehead. He's already runnin' a fever. I'll wait a minute for you."

"Sure, Ma."

Josie hurried into the kitchen.

"You want a slug of whiskey, son?" Mrs. Waters asked.

"I could stand one," Jonas answered.

"Charlie, hand me that bottle."

Waters passed the whiskey to his wife. She held the bottle to Jonas's lips. He took a long swallow.

"That's enough." Mrs. Waters pulled the whiskey away.

Josie returned with a folded towel, dampened with cool water. She placed that on Jonas's forehead.

Jonas managed a wan smile.

"Thanks . . . Josie."

"You're welcome."

"You hold still now, boy," Mrs. Waters ordered. She took another hot towel, and finished washing out the hole in Jonas's side.

"Now comes the tough part," she said. "Charlie, put that rag in this boy's mouth. Son, when the pain gets too awful bad, bite down, hard as you can. Charlie, you hold his shoulders down. Ranger, you keep your hands on his chest. If he starts to move, press down, *hard*. Josie, grab his ankles. Don't let him start kickin' around. Son,

215

I'm gonna douse that wound with red-eye now. You ready?"

Jonas nodded.

"Good."

Mrs. Waters poured a good amount of whiskey directly into the wound. Will and Waters had to fight to hold Jonas down. He clamped his teeth on the knotted rag in his mouth.

"I'm goin' after that slug, now."

Mrs. Waters removed a long, thin-bladed knife from the whiskey-filled pan. She inserted it into Jonas's side, sliding the blade between two of his ribs.

"Don't move," she warned, when Jonas stiffened. "You don't want me to gut you. Bite down harder. The rest of you, make certain he doesn't even twitch."

Mrs. Waters moved the knife gingerly as she searched for the bullet, not wanting to make a slip that could very well kill Jonas. She stopped when she felt the knife hit something solid.

"I found it," she said. "I'll have it out of you in a jiffy, son. Josie, hand me the forceps."

"Yes, Ma."

Josie plucked a pair of forceps from the instrument pan. She handed them to her mother, who inserted them into Jonas's side, sliding them along the knife blade until they reached the bullet.

"Got it!"

She clamped the forceps around the chunk of lead, then pulled them out, followed by the knife. She held up the bullet for Jonas to see.

"There it is. You were damn lucky, son. Not only didn't it break one of your ribs, it didn't go in deep enough to tear up your insides. It's also a stroke of luck a doctor passin' through gave me those forceps. Tryin' to get that bullet out of you with just a knife would've been damn nigh impossible. All I've gotta do now is sew you up, put a poultice on that wound, then bandage it up. After that, rest is what you need. You'll have to let nature take its course. And if you're a prayin' man, asking the Lord to help you heal ain't a bad idea."

"I'm grateful, ma'am."

"T'warn't nothin'. Josie, get my large needle and heavy thread. Dip 'em in the whiskey for me, then I'll stich that wound."

"Sure, Ma."

Josie soaked the needle and thread, then handed them to her mother. Mrs. Waters sliced away several ragged, dead pieces of skin, then sewed the wound's edges together. Lastly, she smeared a foul-smelling poultice on the wound, covered it with a bandage, and tied that in place.

"What you need now is sleep, son," she told Jonas. "Later on, I'll let you have some beef broth. You'll need that to start buildin' up your blood. Charlie, Ranger, carry him into the gentlemen's bedroom. Any travelers spendin' the night, until this boy is feelin' better, will have to sleep on the parlor floor, or in the stage. He can't be disturbed until he's feelin' better."

"Am I gonna . . . make it?" Jonas asked.

"I'm got to be honest, son. I can't promise anything," Mrs. Waters answered. "I don't know how much damage that slug did to your insides. You've lost a considerable amount of blood. You're also running a fever, which means infection is setting in. That's the biggest worry. Until the fever breaks, you're not out of the woods. But you've got a far better chance now than you did when you got here."

Jonas was carried into the men's bedroom, and placed on its sole double bed. He was covered with a sheet and thin blanket. Mrs. Waters gave him another swallow of whiskey to ease his pain, and help him sleep.

"You get as much sleep as you can," she ordered Jonas. "If you need anything, just give a holler."

"Yes, ma'am. I'll do that."

"Mrs. Waters, do you have some blankets, and mebbe a pillow I can borrow, to spread on the floor next to Jonas's bed?" Will asked. "I'd like to stay with him."

"Of course, I do. I'll get you those soon as I fix us somethin' to eat."

"I'm obliged, ma'am."

"It's Louise. Told you that when you came through last time."

"While you're fixin' our meal, I'd best get the gear off those horses the Rangers brought in, then feed and water 'em," Waters said.

"I'll give you a hand," Will said.

"I'm obliged. You can wash up at the trough after we're done."

"Louise, if anythin' happens to Jonas while we're caring for those horses, please let me know."

"I'll send Josie for you. But he's fine, for now."

"*Gracias.*"

Jonas spent four days drifting in and out of a coma, fighting an infection which threatened to overwhelm his body's defenses. Will stayed with him the entire time, unwilling to leave until he was certain Jonas would survive. Sometime in the middle of the fourth night, Jonas's fever finally broke. He awakened with a cry of, "I'm starving."

"Huh? Is that you, Jonas?" Will said, startled out of his sleep.

"Yeah."

Will scrambled to his feet.

"Good to see you awake again, pard. For a couple of days, we thought you weren't gonna make it. This is gonna sound silly, but how are you feelin'?"

"Like a man who's been shot, that's how. Kinda washed out. And one who's bein' starved to death. How long have I been out?"

"Over four days. Hang on. I'll get Louise to fix you up somethin'. She's gonna want to check on your wound, too."

"I'm not goin' anywhere."

"No, I guess not."

Will went to the kitchen to find Mrs. Waters. He returned with her and Josie. Josie carried a bowl of hot beef broth, and a cup of strong tea. Her mother had clean bandages and a tin of ointment.

"You're looking much better, Jonas," Mrs. Waters said, as she placed a hand on his forehead. "Your fever is gone, and your color is much better. I'm going to clean your wound and redress it. Then Josie will feed you."

"I can manage to feed myself."

"Not for a day or two," Mrs. Waters said.

"I don't mind, Jonas," Josie added, with a warm smile, which sent the blood racing through Jonas's veins. She was about his age, with hair the color of honey, and eyes the shade of forget-me-nots. The pink checked gingham robe and white apron she wore over her nightgown failed to completely conceal the curves of her young womanhood.

"I can't win this argument, can I?"

"No, son, you can't," Mrs. Waters said. She started to pull back the sheet and blanket covering

Jonas. Realizing he was naked under the covers, Jonas grabbed the sheet and tugged it back up over his chest. His face turned bright red.

"What's the matter?" Mrs. Waters asked.

"You . . . I . . . it ain't decent, that's what. Not in front of your daughter. You, neither."

"Stuff and nonsense. Who do you think helped me when I was taking the bullet out of you? Who do you think helped get you undressed, and into bed?"

"You mean—"

"Yes. You're not the first injured man whose chest Josie has seen."

"It's more'n my chest that ain't covered."

"Is *that* what you're worried about? No need to be. I'm not lowering the sheet past your waist."

Jonas gave in.

"All right. But if you tug it any lower than that, I'm pullin' it right back up."

Mrs. Waters removed the soiled bandages, and washed off the old dressing.

"You're wound's healing nicely. There's no sign of infection," she said. "A few days' rest and nourishment, and you'll be up and out of that bed. It's gonna be at least two weeks before you can even think about getting on a horse, though."

"I can't take that long. There's more outlaws for me'n Will to round up."

"You don't have any choice, pardner," Will said. "If you break that wound open again, it's liable to get infected, and kill you. Plus, if you don't have your strength back, you won't be any good to me in a long chase, or in any kind of a fight. Like it or not, you're stuck here for a while."

"Don't fret too much, Jonas. *I'll* keep you company," Josie said.

Jonas gave her a wide grin.

"I guess I'll just have to suffer, then."

"Somehow I don't think you'll suffer all that much, son," Mrs. Waters said. "Josie either, for that matter."

Both Josie and Jonas blushed.

Once Jonas's wound was redressed, Josie fed him his broth and tea. Will couldn't help but notice she seemed to leave the spoon in his mouth longer than necessary, with each mouthful. Jonas was just about finished eating when Waters and Eddie came in.

"Jonas, my wife said you were awake, and eating. That's good news, son."

"Yeah, it sure is," Eddie added. "My sister's hardly been able to sleep for frettin' about you. She's barely eaten anything, either."

"Oh, go on with the both of you," Josie said. "I've just been worried about Jonas, that's all."

"Funny, sis. I've never seen you make such a fuss over other hurt men you've nursed," Eddie said. Their father laughed.

"That's enough. Out, all of you," Mrs. Waters

ordered. "That includes you, Will. Jonas needs more rest. We all need to get back to sleep. The sun won't be up for three more hours. Jonas, we'll come back then, if you think you'll be up to it."

"Oh, I'll be up for it," Jonas answered. He was speaking to Mrs. Waters, but his gaze was on Josie. "You can count on that."

Three days later, Jonas and Will were sitting outside, relaxing in the sun. Will had taken up smoking a few months before, so they were both enjoying a cigarette.

"Will, I never did get to tell you, that was a damn fine trick you pulled on those *hombres* who tried to hold up the northbound stage," Jonas said. "I never would've thought of it."

"I was takin' an awful risk, but they had us outnumbered, especially once they gunned down the driver and guard," Will answered. "You did a fine job pickin' up on my plan. If you hadn't, it wouldn't have worked. Of course, I didn't mean for you to make things more real lookin' by actually gettin' yourself shot."

He laughed.

"That wasn't part of my plan, either," Jonas answered, also laughing. "But we've taken a whole passel of *muy malo hombres* out of circulation, for good."

"Too bad there's always more to take their

place," Will answered. "I've got something to tell you."

"What is it?"

"The northbound stage from San Angelo leaves for Sweetwater tomorrow morning. I'll be on it."

"What about me? You ain't leavin' me behind."

"Lemme finish. A few more days rest will do you some good. By now, word has gotten around that we're Rangers. When I reach Sweetwater, I'm gonna pick up our horses, then ride back here. As far as anyone knows, you're still recuperatin'. I'm gonna leave it at that. I also don't want anyone to know where we'll be at. I want folks to think we're still down this way. In fact, we'll be headin' north of Sweetwater. We'll swing wide of any towns between here and there."

"So your goin' to Sweetwater, then comin' back down here, is a decoy. It's to throw the bad guys off the track."

"That's right. Plus, if people think you're still hurt, they'll be lookin' for only one man, me. Always keep 'em guessin', if you want to stay one step ahead of 'em."

"Makes sense. Any particular reason why we're headed north?"

"You recollect the Nolan County sheriff said there was trouble up that way?"

"Yeah, I sure do."

"I've been listenin' to the travelers comin'

through, while you've been doin' nothin' but lyin' in bed, gettin' soft and lazy. You know how folks like to gossip. I've picked up quite a few tidbits about trouble north of Sweetwater, up in the southern Panhandle. We'll stay clear of as many towns as we can on our way. I'd rather no one knows we're in the area until after we arrive, and make a few arrests."

"Hey. That's not all I've been doin'," Jonas protested.

"Oh? Doesn't seem like it to me."

"I've been thinkin' about Miss Josie."

"Josie? What happened to Miss Smithers?"

"She's awful pretty, but Josie's cute as a button. Besides, I don't think I'd want to marry a woman who hides a knife in her skirts."

"That *is* somethin' to think about. You ponderin' about gettin' hitched?"

"Not yet. Just thinkin' about the fun parts of bein' married."

"Her ma and pa might have somethin' to say about that. If you do more'n just thinkin', one of 'em's likely to take a shotgun to you, and finish what those holdup men started."

Jonas sighed.

"I know. And I can't do anythin' until my probation's finished, anyway."

"That's right," Will said. "Dunno about you, but this sun's gettin' hot. I'm gonna head inside."

"Sounds good to me. Mebbe I'll take a nap before supper."

"Best idea I've heard all day," Will said. "Let's go."

14

Three weeks later, Will and Jonas were in the southern area of the Texas Panhandle. They had made several arrests en route, and now were on their way to investigate reports of large cattle rustling and horse thieving gangs. They had stopped to water their horses at Ballard Spring.

"We'll be comin' into Matador before night-fall," Will said. "The town's named after the big Matador Ranch. Its headquarters is just north of here. The outfit started the town, and pretty much controls it, plus everything for miles, in every direction. Lately, there's been homesteaders movin' in, leadin' to some bad blood. It don't help none that the Matador isn't owned by Texans. It's operated by a big Scottish syndicate."

"So we could be runnin' into a bad situation of a big cattle outfit, and their hired guns, tryin' to keep out the homesteaders and small ranchers."

"Yup. The usual method is to try'n buy out the small ranchers, real cheap. If that doesn't work, the threats start. If those don't work, the homesteaders usually find themselves burned out. And, of course, accusin' the homesteaders of bein' rustlers, and hangin' 'em without a trial, happens too."

"Sounds like we're gonna have some fun."

Will gave Jonas a crosswise look.

"You've got a strange idea of fun there, pardner."

Pete lifted his dripping muzzle from the spring, and began munching on the grass.

"You're through drinkin', horse?" Will said. "Then it's time to get movin'. You'll get fed when we reach town."

Matador was a small, unincorporated community. Its sole purpose for existence was to serve the needs of the Matador Ranch. There was no hotel, so Will and Jonas made arrangements to throw down their sleeping bags behind the livery stable. After tending to Pete's and Rebel's needs, they ate at the town's sole café, then went to the Dew Drop Saloon, Matador's only drinking establishment. There was just one patron, a young cowboy at the bar, who was sipping on a whiskey. He nodded to Will and Jonas when they bellied up to the mahogany.

"Evenin', gents."

"Howdy," Will answered, as he and Jonas nodded in return.

The bartender put down the glass he was polishing.

"Howdy, strangers. Welcome to Matador, such as it is. What can I get you?"

"Bottle of rye, and two glasses. Old Crow, if you've got it," Will requested.

"I do. That'll be six bits. Harry's the name."

"Will, and my ridin' pard, Jonas."

Harry put two glasses on the bar, then took a bottle from the shelf, opened it, and poured the glasses brim full. Will tossed two silver dollars on the bar.

"Leave the change there, in case we want more after we finish the bottle," Will said.

"Sure enough."

Harry began singing while he resumed polishing glasses.

With the cowboy the only other customer, and the bartender far less chatty than most of those in his occupation, Will and Jonas were unable to catch up on any local news. About an hour after they'd arrived, a group of eight cowboys, loud and rowdy, entered the bar. The lone cowboy put down his half-finished drink.

"Time for me to call it a night, Harry," he said.

"Culley, you in a hurry to get somewhere?" one of the newcomers asked.

"Just back home, Bedford."

"Thought we told you not to come around here."

"I figured just one drink wouldn't hurt. I was in town to pick up some supplies, anyway. Didn't see any harm in cuttin' the dust from my throat."

"This ain't your town. It's Matador property."

"Things're startin' to change around here,

Bedford. It ain't gonna be long before the Matador won't be able to ride roughshod over the rest of us."

"That'll be the day," Bedford said, snorting. "Don't matter none for you, anyway. If you don't take the ranch's offer, it'll be too late for you."

He put his hand on the butt of his six-gun.

"We'll see," Culley said.

Culley deliberately turned his back on the eight men and walked out of the saloon.

"That *hombre*'s got some sand in his craw," Jonas whispered to Will.

"That might just get him killed," Will answered.

Bedford's gaze settled on Will and Jonas.

"Never seen you two in town before."

"Very observant of you," Will said. "We've never been in this town before."

"You'd better not be thinkin' of settlin' down in these parts. It ain't healthy."

"We're just passin' through. But if me and my pard decided we wanted to claim a homestead parcel here, you'd have a fight on your hands if you tried to stop us."

"Just tryin' to offer some friendly advice. Now, I'd suggest you finish your drinks and get outta here. You're standin' in my place."

"More friendly advice? I don't see anyone's name where I'm standin'," Will said. He deliberately poured more whiskey into his glass.

"There's two of us standing here," Jonas said.

"But I guess you *would* need the space of two men, fat man."

"Why, you damned son of a bitch!" Bedford roared. He charged at Jonas, then swung a roundhouse left at his chin. Jonas easily ducked the blow, and sank his right fist wrist deep into Bedford's soft belly.

With a *whoof* of expelled air, Bedford doubled over. Jonas brought both his hands down on the back of Bedford's neck, dropping him to the sawdust covered floor. One of the other Matador cowboys drove a punch into Jonas's kidney, then grabbed his shoulder, spun him around, and punched him in the left eye. When Jonas staggered back, he shot two quick jabs to the young Ranger's gut. Jonas lowered his head and drove it into the man's stomach. Two of the cowboy's partners came to his aid.

Will was surrounded by the other four Matador hands. He delivered a powerful right to one's chin, breaking his jaw and knocking him out of the fight. The others swarmed over him. Will fought them punch for punch, but their superior numbers were wearing him down. His right cheek was split open, and a bruise was rising along his jaw. A sharp pain in his side indicated one of the cowboys' punches might have cracked a rib. He ducked one punch, absorbed another to his stomach, then hit the closest man square on the nose, breaking it. With a howl of pain, the man fell backward, staggering into his partners.

Will heard a man behind him. He turned to meet the new threat . . . straight into the most solid punch to his gut he'd ever taken. Helpless, all the air knocked out of his lungs, he wrapped his arms around his belly. He gagged on the bile rising in his throat as he pitched to the floor. The last thing he saw before sinking into a pool of black was a whiskey bottle being smashed over Jonas's head.

Will gradually regained his senses, stirred awake by the soft moaning of his partner, in pain.

"Jonas? Jonas!"

"I'm right here, Will. Damn, every inch of my body hurts."

Will opened his eyes, then squinted against the light. The sun was already high in the sky. He and Jonas were in an alley. They were covered with muck, vomit, and horse manure.

"Where the hell are we?"

"Behind the saloon. Dunno how we got here. Last thing I remember is the lights goin' out. How about you, Will?"

Will was lying on his belly, where he had been dumped. He rolled onto his back. Every muscle he owned protested.

"I'm still alive. Barely."

"We should probably get outta here," Jonas said. "If we can even move."

"Yeah." Will forced himself to his feet. He stood for a moment, until the swirling in his head subsided. He squinted at Jonas through his one good eye.

"You look awful, Jonas."

"Well, you don't exactly look so good either, pard. And you smell worse than you look."

"We're gonna have to clean up before we get too far. But it for dang sure ain't gonna be in town," Will said. "We'll get our horses and get back on the trail. I don't feel much like eatin' anyway. My belly hurts too much. Let's retrieve the horses."

Jason, the stable owner, was mucking out stalls when Will and Jonas walked into the barn.

"Jason, where you at?" Will called.

"Out back, dumpin' a load of manure. I was beginnin' to wonder if you fellers were comin' back. Be right with you."

Pushing an empty wheelbarrow, Jason came back inside, then stopped short at the sight of the Rangers.

"What the devil happened to you boys? You tangle with a cougar or somethin'?"

"Yeah. Or somethin'," Jonas said. "Are our horses ready?"

"They sure are. I turned 'em out in the corral. I'll get 'em. Sure are a couple of nice animals. Much too good for a pair of drunken saddle tramps like you *hombres* to be ridin'."

"Just get our horses," Will said.

"Right away. Don't want to put up with you two stinkin' up my barn any longer'n I have to."

Jason went to the corral. He returned leading Pete and Rebel. Rebel backed away from Jonas, while Pete wrinkled his nose and snorted at Will.

"I don't need your comments, Pete," Will said to his horse. He slapped the blanket and saddle on Pete, tied on his bedroll, slid the bit into Pete's mouth and the headstall over his ears. Pete snorted again.

"I can't hardly blame your bronc, mister," Jason said.

"He's a character," Will answered. "Say, do you happen to know where a young cowboy name of Culley lives? About average height, not too lanky, sandy brown hair and light brown eyes. Wears a brown hat with a tan leather band."

"Culley Kinsman? What d'ya want with Culley? He's a decent *hombre*. You ain't lookin' to cause him trouble?"

"Not hardly. If anything, the opposite. We met him at the saloon last night. He lit out when a bunch of Matador cowhands walked in. Seems like mebbe he could use some help."

"Mebbe he could, at that," Jason said. He looked at the guns on Will's and Jonas's hips. "Yessir, just mebbe he could. He runs a small ranch with his pa, about seventeen miles south of here. Take the main trail about ten-eleven miles past Roaring Springs. You'll see a sign on a split trunk cottonwood for the CK Ranch. Turn left. The place is about a quarter-mile down."

"He been havin' much trouble with the Matador?"

"They've been tryin' to force him and his pa out, that's for dang certain. But he's got more troubles than just that. Rustlers and hoss thieves have been stealin' him blind. The Kinsman place is only about ten miles from the Croton Breaks. Once livestock disappears in them breaks, it's nigh impossible to find 'em. Every year, the Matador loses cows in there. Once in a while, they come across one that's four or five years old, but never been branded. It's that easy for a cow critter to hole up in those badlands. That makes it an ideal place for cow thieves to disappear with rustled stock, then move out once the rightful owners give up lookin' for 'em. I hope you're not lyin' to me. Mebbe I've said too much. I'd hate to see anythin' happen to that boy, and his pa."

Will decided to take a chance. He reached in his vest pocket, pulled out his badge, winked, showed it to the hostler, then slid it back in place.

"We're not. We've also got some unfinished business with those Matador ranahans. And we're here to clean out the thieves plaguin' this territory. Just don't let anyone know."

"I never saw anyone but a couple of saddle bums," Jason said.

"Obliged. Jonas, let's git."

Will and Jonas mounted, and walked their horses out of the stable.

"Good luck, and *vaya con Dios*," Jason called after them.

15

Will and Jonas stopped at the old Comanche watering hole of Roaring Springs to clean up, and tend to their hurts.

"These clothes ain't even worth tryin' to save," Will said, as he stripped off his shirt and tossed it into the brush, followed by his underwear and socks. "I'll wash out my denims for now. That'll have to do until I can buy some new ones."

"Mine ain't in much better shape," Jonas answered. "Sure hope I can at least get some of the stink out of 'em."

He and Will washed up in the springs, then dried off, got their spare shirts, socks, and underwear from their saddlebags, and redressed. Jonas built a small fire, over which Will fried bacon and beans, and boiled coffee. Once the food was ready, they tossed their ruined clothes on the fire, and watched them burn.

"I reckon we sure enough lost that fight with the boys from the Matador," Jonas said, as he shoveled a forkful of beans into his mouth.

"We didn't just lose. We got whupped bad," Will asked. "It was a massacre."

"We gonna stand for that, or are we goin' after those sons of bitches?"

"Look at it this way, Jonas. Yeah, we got

whupped, but we made those *hombres* pay the price. One's got a busted jaw, another a broken nose. Once you dropped the leader of the bunch, he never did get back up; leastwise, not that I saw. If we go after 'em, we'll have to take on the ranch's entire crew. Yeah, we would probably go in and make some arrests, but we'd never get any convictions. Pretty much everyone around here depends on the Matador for their livelihoods. They ain't about to go up against that ranch. It's their bread and butter. Sometimes, you've just got to know enough when to chalk up your losses as a lesson learned, and walk away. We've got bigger fish to fry."

"Still sticks in my craw, though."

"Mine too. But the bastard I'd really like to get my hands on is the one who slugged me in the belly. I've taken plenty of gut punches, some awful hard ones, but that's the first time an *hombre* managed to knock me out with just one shot to my belly."

"Uh, Will."

"Yeah, Jonas?"

"I've got somethin' to tell you."

"Go ahead, spit it out."

"The *hombre* who gut-punched you so hard."

"What about him?"

"That was me."

"What'd you just say?"

"It was me. I didn't realize it was you behind

238

me. Last I knew you were still on the other side of the room. I was half-blinded from blood runnin' in my eyes. All I saw was someone takin' a swing at me. I didn't have time to think. I just swung as hard as I could. I'm sorry, Will. I truly am."

"You're sayin' it was *you* who pretty near drove my belly button clean out my backside?"

"I'm afraid so. Dammit, Will. It was an accident. I thought you were one of the Matador *hombres*. Just mebbe, if I hadn't knocked you out, we could've won that fight."

Will shook his head.

"I doubt it. We were both pretty well dead on our feet by then. But boy howdy, I'm beginnin' to wonder how long I'll keep on livin' with you as a pardner. First you nearly break my back when you land on me during the train robbery. Then, you punch me so hard my belly's gonna be black and blue for a month. Next time I turn around, you'll probably shoot me. You're a downright dangerous *hombre*."

"You want to be shut of me? Tell Cap'n Hunter you don't want me as your pardner?"

Will shook his head.

"I can't do that. It would end your probation, and put you behind bars. No, like it or not, we're stuck with each other. Besides, except for when you're tryin' to kill me, you're turning out to be one helluva lawman."

"Next town we hit, I'll buy you a drink to

make up for this, at least a little," Jonas said.

"You can make up for it even more by promisin' never to hit me again. Damn, you pack a wallop. I know one thing. Remember back when we started out on this trip, and you were wonderin' who was faster with a gun, you or me?"

"I sure do. Still wonderin' about that."

"Mebbe someday we'll have a contest, and see once and for all. But I can tell you for certain, you sure as hell can punch a whole lot harder'n me. It felt like I'd been kicked by an iron shod mule when you nailed me."

"There's a knack to it. Somethin' my pa showed me. When we get to feelin' better, I'll teach you the trick."

"It's a deal. Let's finish eatin' and get back on the trail. If Jason's directions are right, we should be at Culley's ranch in a bit more's two hours from now."

"That looks like the cottonwood Jason described, Will," Jonas said, pointing to a large double-trunked tree, which had somehow found a source of water sufficient for its survival in this arid climate. "Don't see any sign for a ranch on it, though."

"There it is, lyin' in the dirt," Will answered. "Looks like someone just tore it down, not long ago. I'm smellin' smoke, too. Something's wrong. C'mon, Pete, let's move."

He dug his heels into the big paint's sides, putting him into a dead run, with Jonas on Rebel right alongside. They rode up on a scene of utter devastation. All that was left of the CK Ranch's buildings were piles of smoldering rubble. Corral fences were flattened, all of the livestock apparently run off.

"Let's see if we can find anyone alive," Will said, as he dismounted. "Then we'll try'n pick up the trail of whoever did this."

Before Jonas could get off Rebel, a rifle bullet split the air just over his head.

"Neither one of you move," Culley Kinsman ordered. He was behind them, standing almost completely hidden, in a narrow gap between two embankments of jumbled rocks and sand. He was protected by the trunk of a large mesquite. "Otherwise, my next bullet'll be plumb in the middle of your back. You on the ground. Step away from that horse, then unbuckle your gun belt. Drop it slow and easy, then raise your hands. The *hombre* still in the saddle. Raise your hands. Soon as your *compadre* sheds his gun, you do the same. Then get off your horse."

"All right, Culley," Will answered. "Jonas, do as he says."

He backed several paces away from Pete, then unbuckled his gun belt and let it drop to his ankles.

"Now you," Culley told Jonas. "One-handed.

241

Then get off that horse and step away from it."

Jonas used his left hand to unbuckle his gun belt, and toss it aside. He dismounted, and walked several feet away from Rebel.

"Now, turn around and face me, both of you. Keep your hands high."

"We ain't lookin' for trouble," Will said, as he and Jonas turned toward the angry, distraught rancher. "We came to palaver with you a spell. Sure didn't expect to find what we did."

"The hell you didn't. You're part of the bunch that killed my father, and burned down my place. Reckon you bastards must've come back to see if there's anythin' worth takin' you missed. I reckon you're both wonderin' why I didn't just shoot you sons of bitches in the back, and be done with it."

"The thought had crossed my mind," Jonas said.

"Because I want to look into your eyes when I kill you. I'm gonna make you sweat, and take my time about it. You're gonna die slow, just like my pa did. I'm gonna put bullets right through your kneecaps. Then I'll stake you out on those smolderin' timbers. You'll roast nice and slow. You're gonna get a taste of Hell before I send you there."

"You gonna give us a chance to say somethin' first?" Will asked.

"I guess so. Only seems right. But talk fast. No tricks, neither."

"No need to worry about that. We're Texas Rangers. My handle's Will Kirkpatrick. My pard's is Jonas Peterson. We're assigned to track down the renegades in these parts. The livery stable owner back in Matador told us you've been havin' lots of trouble with cow thieves. He's the one that told us how to find your spread. We came out here to ask you about that."

"You got any proof of who you are?"

"Got my badge in my vest pocket, and we've both got our commissions in our billfolds."

"Show me that badge, then your papers. Just you. I don't want both of you movin' at the same time. Do it slow. Make one wrong move, and you'll take a slug."

"Agreed. I'm goin' for it now."

Will reached into his pocket, pulled out his badge, and held it up.

"That's fine. Now, your papers."

Will got his billfold, pulled out his papers, unfolded them, and held them up for Culley to see.

"Longer we stay here, the less chance we have of findin' the men who killed your pa," he said.

"All right. I reckon you're who you say you are," Culley said. "Ranger, you can get off your horse. But I'm keepin' my gun on both of you, just in case."

"That's sensible," Jonas said, as he swung out of his saddle.

Leading his gray gelding, Culley came out from cover and drew nearer the Rangers.

"Now I recognize you fellers," Culley exclaimed. "You were in the saloon last night. What the hell happened to you? Appears like you picked a fight with a mad bull, and lost."

"The bunch from the Matador that came in when you left is what happened to us, Culley," Will answered. "They paid a high price for tanglin' with us, but we paid a higher one. You think they did this?"

"I can't say for certain, but I don't think so, Ranger."

"Will. And Jonas."

"Got ya. The Matador's been tryin' to shove people around, and force 'em to sell out, but they ain't pulled any real rough stuff like this, leastwise, not up until now. My pa was still alive when I found him. He told me he didn't recognize any of the raiders. Then he said, 'Good-bye, I'm goin' to Heaven to be with your ma and sisters.' Those were his last words. I'd just finished buryin' him when I heard you fellers ridin' up. Now I'm plumb glad I didn't just shoot you two in the back, like I'd planned. Still don't know why I didn't. Mebbe it was the Lord told me not to."

He stopped, his eyes filling with tears.

"Or your father," Will said.

"I reckon it might've been Pa, at that. We were

always real close. This ranch was my dream, not his. But when my ma and sisters died of the dysentery, he came out from Omaha to help me build it up. Listen, if you're gonna take the trail of the bastards who did this, I'm goin' with you."

"We won't turn down the help, that's for sure," Will answered. "I doubt we'll catch up with 'em before dark, but we can get a start. You can tell us what happened while we ride. We'll just let our horses have a drink, then light out."

A spring gushed from the base of a cliff behind where the CK's house and horse barn had stood. It emptied into a wooden stock tank, from which it overflowed and formed a small creek. The horses were each allowed to drink their full, then the men took off on the trail of the rustlers. The tracks were easy enough to see, a number of cows driven by several men on horseback.

"They headed for the Croton Breaks, Culley?" Will asked, as they rode.

"Sure seems like it," Culley answered. "A man could search for a whole passel of rustlers in those breaks for a month of Sundays, and never find 'em."

"We'll track 'em down. You can bet your hat on it," Jonas said.

"Culley, I take it by the time you got back they were long gone," Will said. "You find anythin' at all that might've given you a clue who they are?"

Culley shook his head.

"I wish I had, but no. I was clear up at the north end of my property, planning a route for a barbed wire fence. They must've hit when I was down in a dry wash, because I didn't hear any gunfire. When I got closer to home, I smelled smoke. I ran ol' Foggy Bottom, here, who's a mighty tough cayuse, almost into the ground, but I was too late. Everything was aflame. I heard my pa cryin' out. He was trapped in the barn. I managed to pull him out, but he was burned real bad, and all shot up besides. Only thing he could tell me was there were at least a dozen men. He said he winged a couple of *hombres*, but not bad enough to knock 'em off their horses. When we do catch up to those sons of bitches, I'm gonna finish what my pa couldn't. Just before Pa took his last breath, I told him I'd run down and kill every one of those *hombres*."

"You think they're working for someone who wants your spread, no matter how they get it, or just a cattle rustlin' outfit?" Will asked.

"There's no way to tell. I've had quite a few offers for my place. The spring where you watered your horses never goes dry. That makes my place worth a lot more than most of the other small ranches around here. But, except for the Matador usin' some rough tactics, none of the other small ranchers or dryland farmers have had any real trouble. Certainly nothin' like what happened to me. Until today. There's been no fires, and no shootin'. If I had to make a bet, I'd wager it's a bunch of rogue cowboys, probably white outlaws and Mexican *vaqueros*, workin' together."

"This close to the Territories, it could be someone workin' in cahoots with some renegade Indians," Jonas said, "Or more likely a crooked Indian agent, stealin' beef from folks around here, and billin' the government, sayin' he bought the meat all legal and proper. It wouldn't be that hard to work up some false invoices. How many cows do you reckon you've lost?"

"I hadn't thought of that, but you could be right," Culley agreed. "As far as cows, just about a hundred, mostly yearlings and two-year-olds. I was just gettin' my herd to where it would start payin' off, soon. Now, I've got nothin' left. No house, no barn, no cows. Those bastards even took my pa from me That's the worst thing they could have done. Now, I've got no kin left."

"We can't do anything about your pa, but we damn sure are gonna get your cows back," Will assured the distraught cowboy. "Look, rustlers generally don't move stolen beef in the daylight. It's too risky. They'll hole up for the day, then move the herd at night. We've only got a bit of daylight left, and I'd say the rustlers are still a couple of hours ahead of us. Even if they've stopped, as I suspect they have, that means there's no way we can catch up with 'em before nightfall. We sure don't want to try'n take 'em durin' the night. Even if we get a miracle on our side, there's bound to be shootin', and that would stampede your cattle. More likely what'd happen is we'd get ourselves shot to ribbons. Or most of the men we're after could just slip away in the dark. Too many things can go wrong."

"I know you've got a plan workin' out in your head, Will," Jonas said.

"Yup. What I propose we do is ride until sundown, then stop for the night."

"But that means those rustlers will be movin' my stolen cows all night, while we're sleepin'," Culley objected.

"Hear me out," Will said. "Cows can only be moved so fast, even by men in a hurry. We can travel a lot faster than those men pushin' your herd, especially on horses fresh from a night's rest. Our broncs traveled a lot more miles today than yours did. They need feed, water, curryin', and rest. I figure we should catch up with your herd sometime tomorrow afternoon. That means we'll get to the rustlers soon before they duck into the breaks, where it'd be a lot more difficult to chouse 'em out of those canyons. We should be able to get close enough before they see us to take 'em by surprise. They probably don't think anyone's on their trail, at this point. The dust your cows throw up will help keep us hidden, too. We'll hang back until they bed the herd for the night, then hit those hombres, hard and fast. Any questions?"

"We gonna give those men a chance to surrender?" Jonas asked.

"If Culley's father's information is right, there's twelve of them, probably all hardened outlaws, most with wanted dodgers on their heads, and three of us. What do you think?"

"We go in shootin'," Jonas answered.

Will nodded his head.

"We go in shootin', unless Culley has any objections."

"Those men killed my pa, and burned down my ranch. I sure as hell don't have any objections."

"Then it's settled. Soon as we come across a likely spot, we'll bed down for the night." Will said. "It'll be a cold camp, of course. Can't even chance someone seein' a small fire, or catchin' a whiff of wood smoke. Let's put a few more miles behind us."

16

Will, Jonas, and Culley came within a half-mile of Culley's stolen herd shortly after ten in the morning the next day. Will instructed his partners to hang back, while he went ahead to scout the situation. He was gone for nearly an hour.

"We were startin' to get worried waitin', Will," Jonas said when he returned. "We were beginnin' to think somethin' had happened to you."

"No, I'm fine. I just wanted to make certain it was the right bunch."

"Is it?" Culley asked.

"It damn sure is. I was able to sneak close enough to catch of glimpse of the brands on some of the cows. It's the CK. Yours."

"Damn sons of bitches," Culley muttered.

"How many are there?" Jonas asked.

"I can't say for certain, but Culley's pa's guess of a dozen or so men looks to be about right."

"So we're outnumbered three to one," Culley said.

"Those aren't bad odds. Me'n Jonas have been up against worse, lots of times. And we're still above ground and upright."

"How're we gonna take 'em?" Jonas asked.

"Like I said yesterday, we'll hang back, and hit 'em shortly after they bed down the herd.

They're just about ten miles past the beginning of the breaks. That must be why they traveled past sunup. They wanted to reach a spot where they wouldn't be out in the open. I imagine they'll push the cows into one of the draws for the rest of the day. It'll be easier for 'em to control the cows if they have 'em blocked in on three sides. Of course, that'll also make it easier for us. If any of those *hombres* make a break for it, they'll have to come right past us. We'll have 'em trapped."

"What about cover?"

"We'll have to wait and see for certain where they stop."

"Makes sense. What do we do in the meantime?"

"We stay right about as far behind that bunch as we are now. When they stop, we stop. We'll give 'em enough time to settle the herd, then move in on 'em."

"Will, don't you mean 'mooove' in on 'em?" Jonas asked, chuckling.

"Jonas, if we weren't so bad outnumbered, I'd gut-shoot you right here and be done with it," Will grumbled. "Culley, before we make our move, I've got a couple of questions for you."

"Go ahead."

"First, are you gonna be able to keep yourself in check? I can't have you goin' off half-cocked, and mebbe spookin' those men, or bringin' 'em down on us before we're ready."

"No worries there. You let me come along with you. I'll follow your orders."

"*Bueno*. What about your horse? Is he spooked by gunfire?"

"Foggy Bottom? Not at all. I hunt off him all the time. Ain't that right, Fog?"

Culley leaned over and patted his gray's neck. The horse nickered.

"How about callin' out to other horses? Is he the talkative type?"

"Not generally, no. But I can't guarantee he won't sound off if he catches the scent of another cayuse."

"You'll have to muzzle him with your bandana before we go in, then. Can't take a chance on him whinnying, and givin' us away."

"Anything else?"

"No. We'll take some time to check our weapons, and get some rest. We're near enough to those rustlers now that we don't have to worry about 'em slippin' away from us. There's a patch of pin oaks a little ways ahead. It'll give us shade, and somethin' for the horses to munch on. We'll stop there."

Two hours later, they were just about in position to attack the gang which had burned Culley's ranch, murdered his father, and stolen his cattle. Will was giving his partners their final instructions.

"Remember, I'm givin' you two minutes to reach the end of that wash. The way it curves around before it reaches the *arroyo* where our men are hidin', no one should see you, unless they happen to look straight down into the wash. Stay under cover until you hear my first shot. Soon as you do, pop up and start pourin' lead into those *hombres*. Make every shot count."

"What if any of 'em want to surrender?" Culley asked.

"If any of that bunch decides to give himself up, I'll eat my hat, without any salt, pepper, or gravy," Will answered. "We know they killed your father, and probably more men, besides. They know they're facin' a noose, or, if they get lucky, life at hard labor in Huntsville."

"Dunno about you boys, but I'd rather hang than spend the rest of my days in Huntsville," Jonas said.

"Same here. Which is why none of those men is gonna give up. They'll go down shootin'. Which means we have to get every damn one of those bastards before they get us. You know how some Indians have a saying that 'It's a good day to die'? Well, I'm tellin' you there's no such thing as a good day to die. Now, let's get this done. Be careful, and good luck."

The two minutes ticked slowly by while Will waited for Jonas and Culley to get in place. The sun was high in the sky, beating down on him.

The air was completely still, not a breeze stirring. The only sounds were the lowing of Culley's stolen cattle, and the occasional chirp of a bird, hiding in the scant shade of the brush. A lizard skittered across the sand. Sweat glistened on Will's brow. It made dark circles under his arms, and soaked the back of his shirt, plastering it to his skin.

"Reckon it's about time, Pete," he said to his paint. "Let's go."

Three men were guarding the mouth of the *arroyo*, two on horseback, the third perched atop a large boulder. That man was leaning against the *arroyo*'s wall, smoking a cigarette. He had his hat pulled down low over his eyes, protecting them from the sun's glare and heat radiating from the rocks.

Will rode as close as he dared, then stopped Pete with a gentle tug on the reins. He lifted his Winchester, and looked at the man on the boulder.

"If you're supposed to be guardin' your pals, you're doin' a damn poor job of it, mister," Will muttered. He shifted his rifle to aim at the nearest man on horseback.

"Texas Rangers! You're surrounded!" Will's voice echoed through the *arroyo*. The man he'd targeted turned toward him, and started to pull his rifle out of its scabbard. Will shot him off his horse, with a bullet in the chest. The man on the boulder jumped up, looking around in confusion.

Before he got his bearings, Will shot him through the gut. He grabbed his middle, jackknifed, tumbled headlong off the boulder, and thudded to the dirt.

The second man on horseback pulled out his rifle and got off one hasty shot at Will, which missed badly. The bullet clipped a wand off an ocotillo several yards to Will's left. Will's return shot hit his target in the side, the slug punching through a rib and into the man's lung. He sagged in the saddle, then slid sideward off his horse. His right foot caught in the stirrup. His panicked horse took off at a gallop, its rider's body dragging and bouncing alongside.

Jonas and Culley had added their fire to Will's, spraying the *arroyo* with a hail of lead. The rest of the rustlers had been gathered around a campfire, eating, when the attack began. Four of them were already sprawled lifeless in the sand.

"Let's get the rest of 'em, Pete," Will yelled. A veteran of many gun battles, Pete knew what was expected of him. He needed no urging to break into a gallop, zigging and zagging to make himself and his rider poor targets, as they raced toward the *arroyo*. Will kept levering and firing his Winchester. He knew the odds of making a hit from the back of a running and twisting horse were practically none, but his shots kept the remaining rustlers busy while Jonas and Culley kept them pinned down, with their withering fire.

Two of the rustlers managed to reach their horses. They jumped into their saddles and spurred the animals mercilessly, in a desperate attempt to escape. Will stopped Pete, took steady aim at one of the oncoming men, and fired. His bullet caught the man dead center, just below the breastbone. He slumped over this horse's neck, then fell to the ground.

The other man got off a shot, which burned along the left side of Will's neck. Jonas and Culley fired simultaneously, putting two slugs into the man's back. He fell, dead before he hit the dirt.

Almost as quickly as it had started, the gunfire stopped. Silence, except for the bawling of the nervously milling cattle, descended on the *arroyo*.

"You fellers all right?" Will asked Jonas and Culley, when they emerged from the wash, leading their horses.

"We're both fine," Jonas answered. "What about you? Looks like you're bleedin' a bit."

"Got stung by a bullet from the last man you boys downed," Will answered. "It's not much. A little salve and it'll be fine. Let's see if any of these *hombres* are still alive."

Will dismounted. Using the barrels of their rifles to roll any rustlers who had landed face-down onto their backs, they checked them for signs of life. They found none.

"I guess that's one cow-thievin', murderin' band who won't ever steal any more cows," Jonas said.

"We got lucky, and they got careless," Will said. "The lookout on the rock was half-asleep. I don't think he even knew what hit him. That gave me a bit more time to pick off the other guards. Then, the rest of 'em being caught settin' around the fire was another big break. It's not often outlaws are that stupid."

"Boy howdy, that's for certain," Jonas said. "But I thought you were just gonna start shootin', without givin' those *hombres* any warning. So why'd you call out 'Texas Rangers' before you fired your first shot?"

"I had to make it legal, didn't I?" Will answered, with a grin.

"Yeah, I reckon you did, at that," Jonas conceded.

They continued to examine the outlaws' bodies.

"I recognize this *hombre*," Will said. "It's Ike Mahoney. He's been in and out of prison for years. Always for cattle or horse stealin'. Looks like he put together a new bunch."

"This one's Montana Dinkins," Culley said. "He got fired from the Matador for abusin' horses. Swore he'd come back and get revenge."

"What're we gonna do with these *hombres*?" Jonas asked. "We sure can't haul 'em all the way back to town, and we dang for certain don't have any way to bury 'em."

257

"Not much we can do," Will said. "We'll drag the bodies to the wash and dump 'em over the side. We could try to collapse the bank onto 'em, but I doubt it would work. I'm not certain it's worth the bother, anyway."

"After what they did to me, I say let the buzzards and coyotes have a feast on those sons of bitches," Culley said.

"Why? What have you got against buzzards and coyotes? Jonas answered. "You want to poison 'em?"

Culley gave a grim laugh.

"Will, are we gonna start back today?" Jonas asked.

"No, I don't think that's a good idea. Those cows are so wound up they're liable to stampede if we try to move them. Our horses can use some rest, too. We'll spend the night here, then start back in the morning."

"That's fine."

After depositing the dead rustlers in the dry wash, Will and his partners looked over Culley's herd. Along with the cattle, the raiders had stolen his *remuda*. One of the horses, a palomino mare, broke away from the others and trotted up to Culley, nickering.

"Sunshine. I never expected to see you again, gal. You don't know how happy this makes me."

"This was my pa's horse," he said to Will and

Jonas. "He spoiled her rotten. At last I've still got one thing that reminds me of him."

"You'll also get to keep the rustlers' horses and gear," Will told him. "It ain't much, but it'll compensate you a little for your losses."

"I appreciate that, Will."

"How about we push those cows farther back into the *arroyo*, then call it a day?" Jonas suggested. "Dunno about you two, but I'm bushed."

"That's a good idea," Will agreed. "Let's git'r done."

17

"These breaks might be one helluva place to find stray cows, but they sure are pretty," Jonas said.

He, Will, and Culley were eating breakfast at sunrise. The sun was bathing the rocks and cliffs of the Croton Breaks, making the orange, yellow, and ochre rocks glow as if they were afire. They stood in stark contrast to the drab, brush and dead grass covered prairie.

"They are," Jonas agreed. "Too bad men like those *hombres* we tangled with yesterday stain spots like this with their ugliness."

"That's why we're paid to stop as many *malo hombres* as we can," Will pointed out.

"Yeah. Some pay. Forty dollars a month, and we've got to supply our own horse, gear, and weapons," Jonas retorted. "All we get from Austin is bullets and grub, for riskin' our necks every damn day."

"You could always go to work for the state in Huntsville instead," Will reminded him. "Guaranteed job, a roof over your head, and three meals a day for the next five years."

"Funny, Will. Real funny."

"If you two are just about finished eatin' and arguin', let's saddle up our horses and get on our way," Culley said. He drained the last of his coffee.

"We *have* dawdled long enough," Will said. He and Jonas dumped the remains of their coffee on the fire, then stamped out the coals, and covered the ashes with sand. They scrubbed the plates and mugs with more sand, and put them back in their saddlebags. They retrieved their horses, got the gear on them, and mounted. With only three men to handle nearly a hundred cows, they let the herd boss, a brindle cow, lead the cattle, rather than one man riding point. Will and Jonas took up the flanks, while Culley rode drag, where he'd catch more of the dust thrown up by the cows' hooves than either of his partners. The cattle moved along willingly enough, since the grazing in the *arroyo* had been sparse.

They had gone about two miles when Will happened to look back. He reined his paint to a halt, then called out to Jonas and Culley.

"Whoa, Pete. Jonas, Culley, hold up a minute."

With no one driving them, the cattle also stopped, dropping their heads to graze. Will rode over to his partners.

"Somethin' wrong, Will?" Jonas asked.

"There sure is. We're bein' followed. Take a look."

"Boy howdy, we sure are," Culley said. Not far behind the herd a large dust cloud marred the azure sky. It grew larger as the riders drew nearer.

Will took out his field glasses and stood up in his stirrups to get a closer look.

"Think it's trouble, Will?" Jonas asked.

"I wouldn't bet against it. There's no use in tryin' to outrun whoever it is. We'll wait here until we can see who they are."

Will kept his glasses trained on the horizon. It wasn't long before he could make out a large group of horsemen. A moment later, he could pick out individuals. He put down his field glasses and cursed.

"Damn."

"What've you got, Will?" Jonas asked.

"Looks like about twenty riders. Can't tell for certain. But they sure ain't comin' by just to say howdy."

"Rustlers?" Culley asked.

Will shook his head.

"I've got no idea who the hell they are. Look like a bunch of soldiers and Indians, ridin' together. Seems to be a white civilian leadin' the outfit. Damned if I can figure it out. But we'd better think of somethin', quick. We're sittin' ducks out here in the open."

To punctuate his words, two of the riders unshipped their rifles, and sent long distance bullets whistling over the herd. Will looked at the surroundings.

"Culley, sorry, but we can't worry about your cows right now. See that trail up into the breaks?

It climbs steep, and fast. If we can make it to the top, we should be able to hold off those hombres until they quit, and turn back. Mebbe we'll get lucky, and they'll only take the cows, and forget about us."

He didn't need to finish his thoughts. Even with controlling the high ground, and with solid cover, sooner or later, the superior numbers of the enemy would probably overwhelm them. And there was no way the apparent rustlers would leave any witnesses behind.

The Rangers and Culley put their horses into a gallop, streaking across the open ground. By the time they reached the base of the cliffs, the horses were at a dead run. Several of their pursuers had closed to within rifle and arrow range. Bullets whined around the fleeing men. Pete screamed in pain when a rifle bullet scoured a path along his left hip. He slowed for a moment, then resumed his pace. "You two go ahead," Will shouted. "I'll cover you from back here. When you get to the gap near the top, swing in there. That's as good a place as any to make our stand."

Leaning low over their horses' necks, Will, Jonas, and Culley made a desperate run for safety. Pete stumbled and nearly went down when an arrow buried itself in his right flank. Will hauled back on the reins, keeping his horse's head up. Pete staggered, regained his footing, and continued running, albeit at a much slower pace. Will was falling farther and farther behind as Pete struggled, the paint's breathing labored. Blood streaked his hip and dripped from the wound in his flank. Reluctantly, Will took his reins and slashed them across Pete's rump, urging him on. His horse managed to find a bit more speed.

Jonas and Culley reached the gap where the trail leveled off. It was protected by two rock pinnacles on the right, as well as a rough, slanted rocky shelf. The left was a steep embankment of jumbled boulders. They swung behind the pinnacles and dismounted. Each grabbed his Winchester. Culley climbed halfway up the shelf, standing ready to shoot the nearest pursuers, as soon as he had a clear shot. Jonas had to hang onto Rebel's bridle to control the panicked bay. Rebel danced sideways, jamming Fog between his right side and the rock wall. Will rolled off Pete as the paint galloped past.

"Get down, Culley!" he shouted, realizing Culley was skylined, exposed to enemy bullets. He dove at Culley to shove him aside, but was too late. A bullet tore through Culley's thigh, dropping him to one knee.

"How bad you hit?" Will asked.

"Got me in the leg. Think it went on through," Cody answered. "I can still fight. This here's a good spot." He dropped to his belly, and crawled to the top of the shelf. He took two quick shots at the oncoming horsemen. Two of them dropped from their saddles.

Jonas had gotten his frightened horse under control. He squeezed into the narrow space between the rock pinnacles. From here, he could lean out and have a wide field of fire, while protected by the solid granite walls. Will, for his part, snuggled into a nest of boulders on the left side of the trail. As long as their ammunition held out, they could hold off an army from this natural fortress.

Three Indians charged up the narrow trail. Will took aim at the amulet one wore hanging from a leather thong around his neck. The stone hung directly over the Indian's heart. Will pulled the trigger. His bullet struck in the center of the amulet, shattering it and driving pieces of stone into the Indian's heart, along with the bullet. The Indian let out a cry of defiance as he fell from his horse. Jonas shot one of the others in the belly, doubling him over. The Indian rode out of the fight, mortally wounded. Culley tried for the third Indian, but missed. Will shot the Indian through the head. The remaining raiders stopped, and retreated, gathering at the base of the trail, just out of rifle range.

"What d'ya think they're up to?" Culley asked.

"They're tryin' to regroup," Will answered. "Probably tryin' to figure out if there's a way they can get behind us."

The outlaws carried on a conversation for several minutes. The white man in civilian clothing, holding a rifle with a white cloth tied to its barrel, broke off from the group and rode partway up the hill.

"You men up there. This is Harlan Garrity, Indian agent for the Kiowa reservation in the Territories. We were supposed to meet the men who procure beef for us. Instead, we found them dead, murdered. Our promised cattle were nowhere to be found. We followed their tracks, and it seems you have taken possession of them. That means you are guilty of cattle rustling and murder. I demand you surrender immediately. You will be escorted by the United States Cavalry soldiers accompanying me to Federal custody."

"Mr. Garrity, this is Texas Ranger Will Kirkpatrick. The men with me are my partner, Jonas Peterson, and the owner of the CK Ranch, Culley Kinsman. Those men who you claim 'procured' those cows stole them from Mr. Kinsman's ranch, after burning it down and killing his father, in cold blood. When they resisted arrest, we had no choice but to gun them down. As far as being taken into custody, I'm placing you under arrest for receiving stolen property, and as an accessory to murder and arson. Same goes for all the men with you. I'm certain, once the federal authorities investigate, you'll also be charged with defrauding the United States Government.

So, *you* can give yourselves up, or die here today. It's your choice."

Garrity gave a short, derisive laugh.

"Are you insane, Ranger? Even allowing for the men you've killed here, we still have you outnumbered three to one. We have the numbers to overrun you."

"Tryin' to get at us is just plain suicide," Will answered. "You might want to think about that."

"So you have no intention of surrendering?"

"Not one ounce."

"Then prepare to meet your Maker. And may God have mercy on your souls."

Garrity returned to the rest of his men. He ordered a mass charge up the hill.

As Will had warned, it was a suicide mission. Soldiers and Kiowas alike fell with Ranger bullets in their bodies. The survivors retreated, regrouped, and charged again. One of the Kiowas released an arrow from his bow. It struck Will at an angle, high on the left side of his chest, the barb exiting from his armpit. His left arm useless, Will stretched out on his belly, pushing his rifle in front of him. One-handed, he resumed shooting. More men went down. The few survivors turned to flee. Will, Jonas, and Culley put bullets in their backs. The cries of the wounded and dying drifted on the breeze.

"Looks like they're finished, Will," Jonas said. "How bad you hurt?"

"Bad enough I can't do much," Will answered. "You're gonna have to go down and check those men. Any of 'em that're still alive, we'll haul back to Sweetwater."

"I can give you a hand, Jonas," Culley offered.

"Are you certain?"

"Sure. I can use my rifle as a crutch."

"I've got a better idea," Jonas said. "I'll help you and Will on your horses. We'll ride down there together."

"I've gotta see how bad Pete's hurt, first," Will said.

"Lemme give you a hand," Jonas replied. He helped Will to his feet. Will whistled for his horse. Pete trotted up to him, followed by Rebel and Foggy Bottom. Pete put his muzzle in Will's cupped hand and nickered.

"I know you're hurt, pard," Will told his paint. "Lemme see how bad."

To Will's relief, the bullet slash across Pete's hip was minor, and would heal with no difficulty. It had already stopped bleeding. The arrow in his horse's flank was more serious. It would need to be removed, hopefully without much further damage.

"How is he?" Culley asked.

"I think he'll be all right, once I get that arrow out of him," Will answered. "That'll have to wait until we take care of those *hombres* down below."

"Down below, sayin' howdy to Satan, is

probably where most of 'em already are," Jonas said. "Let's go find out."

He helped Will and Culley onto their horses. They rode slowly back down to level ground, where Will and Culley dismounted. Feeling weak and about to faint, Will laid down, while his partners examined the remains of the outlaws.

Harlan Garrity was still alive, suffering from two bullet wounds, which were serious, but survivable, providing infection didn't set in. Two of the soldiers and one Kiowa were also still alive. Jonas made certain each man was unarmed and secured, then turned his attention to Will and Culley.

"I can patch myself up until we get to my place," Culley told Jonas. "I just need some whiskey to pour into this wound, then I'll tie a bandana around my leg and it'll be fine. You'd better see to Will."

"Not until I take care of Pete first," Will said. He pushed himself to his feet, walked over to his horse, and got a tin of salve, along with a clean rag, from his saddlebags.

"I know this is gonna hurt, pal," he told Pete, stroking the horse's rump. "Just don't kick me."

Pete whickered, and tossed his head.

Will grasped the arrow's shaft with both hands. Slowly, he pulled it from Pete's flank. Blood ran from the wound, but to Will's great relief, there was no spurting, which would have indicated a severed artery. Will wiped away blood, coated the wound with salve, and patted Pete's neck.

"Good boy. You'll be just fine. But I'm gonna have to use another horse until you heal up."

Pete snorted, placed his muzzle in the small of Pete's back, and shoved him, hard.

"I don't care if you're jealous, horse," Will said. "I'm not gonna chance cripplin' you up by ridin' you while you're hurt."

"Speakin' of being crippled up, you'd better let me remove that arrow in your chest," Jonas said.

"Yeah, I reckon you're right," Will agreed. "Best thing to do is break off the shaft, then pull out the rest where it came out through my side."

Jonas had Will sit against a rock. Will put his neckerchief in his mouth to bite down on against the pain. Jonas snapped off the arrow's shaft and tossed it away. He lifted Will's arm, grasped the arrow just behind its head, and pulled it free.

"You doin' all right, Will?"

"Just fine and dandy."

"Sure, you are."

Jonas removed Will's shirt, wrapped a bandage around his chest, then slid the shirt back on. He fashioned a sling for Will's arm out of his own bandanna.

"Soon as I patch up those renegades, you want to get started home, Will? We've still got a few hours of daylight left. Or would you rather rest for a spell?"

"No, we'll ride on out. Culley, I'm afraid we'll have to leave your cows behind. Ain't none of us in shape to move a herd, plus they'd hold us up too long."

"I already figured that out, Will. This is still open range, so I can hire a few men to round 'em up and bring 'em home. With luck, I won't lose too many."

"Will, Culley, you both rest while I tend to the others. Then we'll head on out," Jonas said.

18

Will and Culley were in the Sweetwater Sheriff's Office. With them were United States Deputy Marshals Jules Croteau and Clancy Sedgewick.

"You Rangers did a fine job," Croteau said. "We'd been suspicious of Harlan Garrity for some time now. It made little sense, him not having beef brought directly to the reservation. We were trying to build a case against him, and his partners."

"He was probably afraid someone would recognize Ike Mahoney, or one of his men," Will said.

"It doesn't matter. The two soldiers you brought in are singing like canaries. They're hoping to avoid the firing squad," Sedgewick answered. "Not that it's very likely. As far as the Kiowa, he won't say a word. He'll most likely be executed without talking. It's just a shame so many men died, and that you and Mr. Kinsman were hurt."

"And Culley's father murdered," Will reminded him.

"Yes, that's so. We'll be staying the night. If you'd like to join us for supper, the government's paying," Sedgewick offered.

"The government's paying? We'll be there," Will said.

Will and Jonas had obtained a hotel room while they recuperated, and awaited new orders from Captain Hunter. They were halfway to the hotel when the Western Union messenger hurried up to them.

"Got a wire just come in for you, Rangers," the boy said. He handed Will a yellow flimsy. Will took a nickel from his pocket and handed it to the youngster.

"Thanks, son."

"No, thank you, Ranger."

Will unfolded the paper and read the message.

"Well, I'll be damned," he muttered.

"What? Are you gonna read it to me, or do I have to rip it out of your hands?" Jonas asked.

"We've got orders. I still can't quite believe my own eyes. Instead of bein' sent back to our company, Cap'n Hunter's decided to establish a Ranger post, right here in Sweetwater. And we're the two men who are gonna man it."

"You're joshin' me."

"No, I ain't. Read it for yourself."

Will handed the paper to Jonas, who quickly scanned its contents.

"Well, if this don't beat all. Now I'll be able to call on Miss Smithers."

"Pamela Smithers? I thought you were 1... ested in Josie Waters?"

"There's no reason a feller can't court two ladies," Jonas said, grinning.

"You're plumb loco. I'd rather be back in the Croton Breaks, fighting all those outlaws, than be in your boots if those two women found out you were seein' both of 'em, behind each other's back. They'd tear you to pieces."

"Yeah, but think of the fun I'll have in the meantime."

"I've got a suggestion for you. Why not add Melissa Miller to your little harem?"

Jonas shot a backhanded slap to Will's belly.

"Now, in her case, I'd rather take on those outlaws."

"Coward," Will said.

"That's right," Jonas answered.

"Tell you what," Will said. "Let's get haircuts, shaves, and baths before we meet the marshals. After all, if you happen to run into any of your lady friends, you don't want to stink like horses, sweat, and manure. I hear tell women go crazy for an *hombre* wearin' bay rum."

"Now you're talkin', Will. Lead the way."

Author's Note

Miss Hattie's bordello was actually in operation from 1902 to 1952, when it was shut down by the Texas Rangers. It is still in existence today as "Miss Hattie's Bordello Museum." I have moved back its years of operation for the purposes of this story.

About the Author

Jim Griffin became enamored of the Texas Rangers from watching the TV series, Tales of the Texas Rangers, as a youngster. He grew to be an avid student and collector of Rangers' artifacts, memorabilia, and other items. His collection is now housed in the Texas Ranger Hall of Fame and Museum in Waco.

His quest for authenticity in his writing has taken him to the famous Old West towns of Pecos, Deadwood, Cheyenne, Tombstone, and numerous others. While Jim's books are fiction, he strives to keep them as accurate as possible within that realm.

A graduate of Southern Connecticut State University, Jim now lives in Keene, New Hampshire when he isn't traveling around the West.

A devoted and enthusiastic horseman, Jim bought his first horse when he was a junior in college. He has owned several American Paint horses. He is a member of the Connecticut Horse Council Volunteer Horse Patrol, an organization which assists the state park Rangers with patrolling parks and forests.

Jim's books are traditional Westerns in the best sense of the term, portraying strong heroes with good character and moral values. Highly reminiscent of the pulp westerns of yesteryear, the heroes and villains are clearly separated.

Jim was initially inspired to write at the urging of friend and author James Reasoner. After the successful publication of his first book, *Trouble Rides the Texas Pacific*, published in 2005, Jim was encouraged to continue his writing.

Website: www.jamesjgriffin.net